Jessica's Grandest Scheme . . .

In the kitchen, Jessica was bubbling with excitement. "I've got it, Elizabeth!" she whispered loudly.

"Got what?" Elizabeth asked, taking the ice cream from the freezer.

"An idea! A stroke of genius! Look, the Steeles need somebody to watch Chrissy. We need to borrow a little sister or brother to prove to Mom and Dad how much help we'd be if we had a baby in the family. It's *perfect*!"

Elizabeth stared at Jessica. She wondered if she'd heard right. "Are you suggesting that *we* keep Chrissy?"

Jessica clapped her hands. "Exactly!"

"Well, Chrissy is sweet," Elizabeth agreed as she spooned out some ice cream. "But it would be a lot of work, Jessica. We'd have to take her to school and pick her up and put her to bed every night—"

"But that's why it's so perfect! Its *loads* of work. And you and I are going to do every bit of it! This is my grandest scheme ever!"

Elizabeth put down the spoon. "Except for one small flaw."

"What's that?" Jessica asked.

"If you don't do your share of taking care of Chrissy," she said bluntly, "I'll end up with double the work!"

Bantam Books in the SWEET VALLEY TWINS series
Ask your bookseller for the books you have missed

#1 BEST FRIENDS
#2 TEACHER'S PET
#3 THE HAUNTED HOUSE
#4 CHOOSING SIDES
#5 SNEAKING OUT
#6 THE NEW GIRL
#7 THREE'S A CROWD
#8 FIRST PLACE
#9 AGAINST THE RULES
#10 ONE OF THE GANG
#11 BURIED TREASURE
#12 KEEPING SECRETS
#13 STRETCHING THE TRUTH
#14 TUG OF WAR
#15 THE OLDER BOY
#16 SECOND BEST
#17 BOYS AGAINST GIRLS
#18 CENTER OF ATTENTION
#19 THE BULLY
#20 PLAYING HOOKY
#21 LEFT BEHIND
#22 OUT OF PLACE
#23 CLAIM TO FAME
#24 JUMPING TO CONCLUSIONS
#25 STANDING OUT
#26 TAKING CHARGE
#27 TEAMWORK
#28 APRIL FOOL!
#29 JESSICA AND THE BRAT ATTACK
#30 PRINCESS ELIZABETH
#31 JESSICA'S BAD IDEA
#32 JESSICA ON STAGE
#33 ELIZABETH'S NEW HERO
#34 JESSICA, THE ROCK STAR
#35 AMY'S PEN PAL
#36 MARY IS MISSING
#37 THE WAR BETWEEN THE TWINS
#38 LOIS STRIKES BACK
#39 JESSICA AND THE MONEY MIX-UP
#40 DANNY MEANS TROUBLE
#41 THE TWINS GET CAUGHT
#42 JESSICA'S SECRET
#43 ELIZABETH'S FIRST KISS
#44 AMY MOVES IN
#45 LUCY TAKES THE REINS
#46 MADEMOISELLE JESSICA
#47 JESSICA'S NEW LOOK
#48 MANDY MILLER FIGHTS BACK
#49 THE TWINS' LITTLE SISTER

Sweet Valley Twins Super Editions
#1 THE CLASS TRIP
#2 HOLIDAY MISCHIEF
#3 THE BIG CAMP SECRET

Sweet Valley Twins Chiller Editions
#1 THE CHRISTMAS GHOST
#2 THE GHOST IN THE GRAVEYARD
#3 THE CARNIVAL GHOST

SWEET VALLEY TWINS

The Twins' Little Sister

Written by
Jamie Suzanne

Created by
FRANCINE PASCAL

A BANTAM SKYLARK BOOK
NEW YORK • TORONTO • LONDON • SYDNEY • AUCKLAND

RL 4, 008–012

THE TWINS' LITTLE SISTER
A Bantam Skylark Book / June 1991

Sweet Valley High® and Sweet Valley Twins are registered trademarks of Francine Pascal

Conceived by Francine Pascal

Produced by Daniel Weiss Associates, Inc.
33 West 17th Street
New York, NY 10011

Skylark Books is a registered trademark of Bantam Books, a division of Bantam Doubleday Dell Publishing Group, Inc. Registered in U.S. Patent and Trademark Office and elsewhere.

ISBN 0-553-15899-6

Published simultaneously in the United States and Canada

Bantam Books are published by Bantam Books, a division of Bantam Doubleday Dell Publishing Group, Inc. Its trademark, consisting of the words "Bantam Books" and the portrayal of a rooster, is Registered in U.S. Patent and Trademark Office and in other countries. Marca Registrada. Bantam Books, 666 Fifth Avenue, New York, New York 10103.

PRINTED IN THE UNITED STATES OF AMERICA

OPM 0 9 8 7 6 5 4 3

*The Twins'
Little
Sister*

One

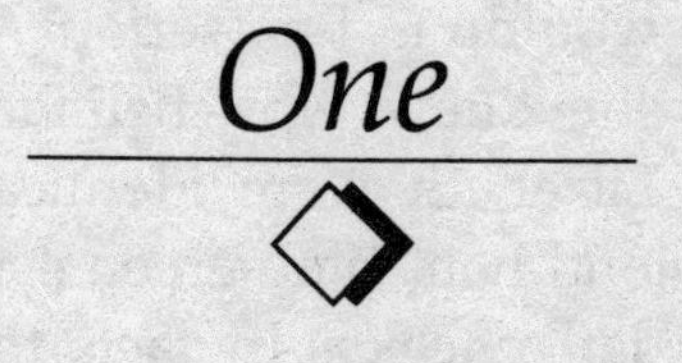

"Isn't he just the *cutest* guy you've ever seen?" Jessica Wakefield asked her twin sister.

Elizabeth laughed. "The last I heard, Aaron Dallas was the cutest guy you'd ever seen," she teased. "What's Aaron going to say when he hears you have your eye on someone else?"

Jessica giggled and looked back down at Belinda Layton's baby brother, Billy, asleep in his crib. She sighed and covered him with a soft blue blanket. "I just *love* babies. I wish we had one."

Belinda smiled. "You might not feel that way at five o'clock in the morning, Jessica. That's the time Billy likes to have his first bottle and get his diaper changed."

"I wouldn't care," Jessica said defiantly. "If

we had a baby as cute as Billy, I'd get up every single morning."

Belinda hooted. "If I know you, Jessica, you'd last about a week. Then it would be Elizabeth's turn—forever!"

"No it wouldn't! I'm serious," Jessica protested. But she knew why Belinda had said it. Jessica and Elizabeth were identical twins, with long, silky blond hair, blue-green eyes, and a dimple in their left cheeks. In fact, they looked so much alike that when they wanted to, they could even fool their friends. The only way to tell them apart was by their very different personalities.

Jessica was always eager for fun and adventure, and she loved the time she spent with her exclusive group of friends, the Unicorns. They gossiped nonstop about boys, rock stars, and the latest fashions. The Unicorn Club consisted of only the prettiest, most popular girls at Sweet Valley Middle School, and they considered themselves superior. In fact, they always wore something purple, the color of royalty. Jessica loved the Unicorns because they all cared about the same thing—having fun!

Elizabeth liked to have fun, too, and she enjoyed spending time with her best friend, Amy Sutton. Unlike Jessica, she didn't have much use for the Unicorns. She thought most of them were snobbish and self-centered, except for Belinda Layton, Mary Wallace, and Mandy Miller. Elizabeth was the older twin, by four minutes, and she was also the more serious and responsible of the two. While Jessica spent most of her time talking about boys, Elizabeth spent her free time writing for *The Sweet Valley Sixers,* the class newspaper she and her friends had founded.

Regardless of their differences, the twins were very close. No matter what kind of a mess Jessica got into, she could always depend on Elizabeth to bail her out. And Elizabeth knew that while Jessica's schemes sometimes got both of them into trouble, she could always count on her twin's loyalty.

"Belinda's right, Jess," Elizabeth teased. "You'd be pretty good at taking care of a baby for a day or two. But then you'd get tired of it. Somebody else would have to do all the work."

Jessica smoothed Billy's hair and watched him snuggle into his blanket. "Well, you're wrong," she insisted. "C'mon, Elizabeth, don't you think it would be terrific to have a little brother or sister?"

"I think it'd be terrific to have a baby in the family," Elizabeth answered. "But I don't think there's much chance of talking Mom into it. She and Dad are pretty definite about three kids being enough."

"My mom and dad decided to wait until I was old enough to help out before they had another baby," Belinda said. She grinned proudly as the three girls went down the stairs to the kitchen. "They say that they never could have managed Billy without my help. Pretty soon Mom will be going back to work, and if I weren't around, they'd have to pay somebody to do all the things that I do to help."

"You see, Elizabeth?" Jessica said triumphantly. "I was right. Mom and Dad are probably just waiting until they think we're old enough to help before they have another baby." She paused thoughtfully. "Maybe we should—"

Elizabeth looked at Jessica suspiciously. "You're not planning to try and talk Mom and Dad into having another baby, are you?"

"I wouldn't do anything as immature as that," Jessica said, offended. "Anyway, it's too obvious. It wouldn't work. What we need to do is to *show* them."

"Show them what?" Belinda asked.

"Show them how responsible we are, of course," Jessica replied, opening a soda. "Show them how much help we'd be if we had a baby in the family."

Elizabeth chuckled. "That might be a little

hard to do. We don't *have* a baby, remember? We'd have to borrow one to demonstrate with."

"Hey, that's not a bad idea," Jessica said. She glanced at Belinda. "Belinda, how about—"

"Forget it, Jessica. You're *not* borrowing Billy, if that's what you have in mind!"

"Don't panic, Belinda," Jessica said, and sighed regretfully. Borrowing Belinda's brother was exactly what she'd had in mind. "We'll come up with something."

"Well, good luck, Jess," Elizabeth said, laughing. "This time you've got a *big* job on your hands!"

Amy Sutton had a big job, too. She was on her way to finish it up when she ran into Jessica and Elizabeth on Friday afternoon.

Elizabeth's eyebrows shot up in surprise when she saw her friend pushing a big wheelbarrow. "Amy," she asked, "what are you doing with that?"

Amy looked proudly at the bulging plastic bag that completely filled the wheelbarrow. "I've been collecting aluminum cans for three weeks. The bag was so full I couldn't carry it."

Jessica wrinkled her nose. "What are you doing with a bunch of smelly old cans?"

"I'm taking them to the recycling center," Amy explained. "I'm going to sell them to get money to buy a pair of soccer tickets for my parents. Their wedding anniversary is next Saturday."

"Do you think you've got enough cans?" Elizabeth asked. "Soccer tickets are kind of expensive."

"Thirty-four dollars," Amy replied. She grinned. "I've never bought them anything that expensive. They're going to be very impressed. I've already got some money saved up," she said confidently. "And I've got a lot of cans. Two hundred and twenty-four, to be exact. I mashed them down so they'd take up less room. Anyway, their anniversary isn't for another eight days. If I don't have enough money, I can always collect more cans. Or I can do something else."

"You could have a cookie sale," Jessica suggested. "Or you could babysit."

Amy shook her head. "I don't have much baking experience," she said. "And I already put up some signs for babysitting, but nobody's called me. I think I'll stick with collecting cans. Do you guys want to come to the recycling center with me? There'll probably be enough money left over for ice cream."

Jessica shook her head. "I've got to get home and call Lila about going shopping tomorrow."

"I'll come," Elizabeth volunteered. She and

Amy waved goodbye to Jessica and headed toward the recycling center.

The man at the center took Amy's cans and weighed them. Then he counted out some money.

"Two dollars and twenty-four cents?" Amy asked disbelievingly, looking at the change in her hand. "Hey, wait! There must be a mistake!"

"Aluminum cans don't weigh much," the man said, shrugging. "But come back when you've got more."

Amy turned away, disappointed. She'd spent three weeks collecting cans, and she'd earned only a little over two dollars! At that rate, it would take her *months* to save enough for the soccer tickets, even with the money she'd already saved.

Elizabeth shook her head. "I don't know, Amy. Maybe a cookie sale isn't such a bad idea after all."

"Maybe," Amy said slowly, "although I'm not much of a baker." She brightened. "But you're good, Elizabeth. If you'd help me bake tomorrow morning, we could hold the sale in the afternoon, in front of my house. I'm sure we could make ten dollars, anyway. Then I could think of some way to earn the rest of the money after school next week."

Elizabeth nodded. "Sure, I'll help."

"Great. Then let's take this money and hit the supermarket!"

When Jessica got home she headed for the kitchen to make a sandwich before she called Lila. She found her brother, Steven, there with a friend, slicing the last of the Swiss cheese.

"Don't eat *all* of that, Steven," Jessica warned. "There won't be any left for me!"

"Tough luck, shrimp," Steven said as he cut another slice. "Chad and I got here first. We just came from basketball practice, and we're starved."

"I'll have peanut butter if your sister wants Swiss cheese," Steven's friend offered.

Jessica looked at the boy with surprise. She recognized him from the Sweet Valley High basketball team. His name was Chad Lucas, and he was a superstar. What was more, he was terrific-looking, with curly blond hair and intense blue eyes. And right now he was handing her the Swiss-cheese sandwich he had made for himself. It had a pickle and mustard on it, just the way she liked it.

"I can't believe it," Steven said, shaking his head. "You're letting my baby sister take your sandwich?"

"She's not taking it, I'm giving it to her," Chad said, smiling. "And she doesn't look like a *baby* sister to me," he added.

Steven groaned. "Can it, Chad. She'll think you're flirting with her."

Chad's grin widened. "What's wrong with a little flirting?" he remarked casually.

Jessica tossed her head. "I accept the sandwich, *and* the compliment." She tried to sound cool and casual, but inside she was full of butterflies. Chad Lucas was flirting with *her!* She went to the refrigerator and got out the peanut butter and a jar of grape jelly. A minute later she handed Chad a sandwich.

"Thanks, Jess," Chad said. "That is your name, right?"

"Actually, it's Jessica," she replied in her most grown-up voice. She poured a glass of milk for Chad.

Steven grabbed the milk carton from his sister and straddled a kitchen chair. "Hey, Jessica, why don't you get lost, huh?"

Jessica lifted her chin. "Steven, why don't *you* grow up?" She took a bag of potato chips out of the cupboard and poured some onto a plate. Smiling brightly, she put the plate in front of Chad.

Steven frowned at his sister. It was obvious that he wanted her to leave. But Jessica knew he wouldn't make a big deal about it in front of Chad. Jessica sat down at the table and took a bite of her sandwich. She listened while Chad and

Steven talked about basketball and things that were going on at Sweet Valley High. After a few minutes, she tuned out and concentrated on Chad.

For a moment she let herself imagine what fun it would be to sit on a beach blanket beside Chad, sipping a soda and letting him spread suntan lotion all over her shoulders. A dreamy smile played at the corners of her mouth as she thought how her friends Ellen Riteman and Lila Fowler would flip when they saw her. Then she came back to earth with a thud. It was an impossible dream. Chad was Steven's friend. Besides, there was Aaron Dallas to consider. After all, she was Aaron's girlfriend. They'd already had two dates. Well, not dates, exactly, because her mother and father thought she was too young to date. But all the Unicorns considered them a couple, and Caroline Pearce had even written a piece about them in her gossip column in *The Sweet Valley Sixers.* Was it fair to Aaron for her to be thinking about another boy?

Jessica tuned back in to the boys' conversation. "I guess you've heard about Joe Howell's party," Steven was saying to Chad.

Jessica already knew about the party, because her friend Janet, an eighth grader and president of the Unicorns, was Joe's sister. Janet was giving the party, too.

"Sure," Chad said, finishing his milk. "A week from tonight. Are you going?"

Steven nodded. "Wouldn't miss it," he said.

Jessica got up and brought a bag of cookies to the table. Chad looked at her. "I guess you're going to the party, too," he remarked. "I heard that Joe's sister is inviting her friends."

Jessica nodded, excitement growing inside her. Chad was actually asking her if she was going to the party! "Yes, I'm going," she said, as coolly as possible.

"Maybe I'll see you there, then," Chad said as he stood up. "I have to get going, Steven," he said. "Thanks for the peanut butter and jelly sandwich."

Steven shrugged. "You *could* have had Swiss cheese."

"Yeah," Chad answered, and smiled at Jessica. "But this way I got a cute girl to make me a sandwich, pour me some milk, and set me up with chips and cookies. What more could a guy want?"

Steven snorted, but Jessica hardly heard him. Chad had called her "cute." There was no doubt about it, Chad *liked* her. Jessica said goodbye and raced upstairs to the phone. She couldn't wait to tell Lila about *this!*

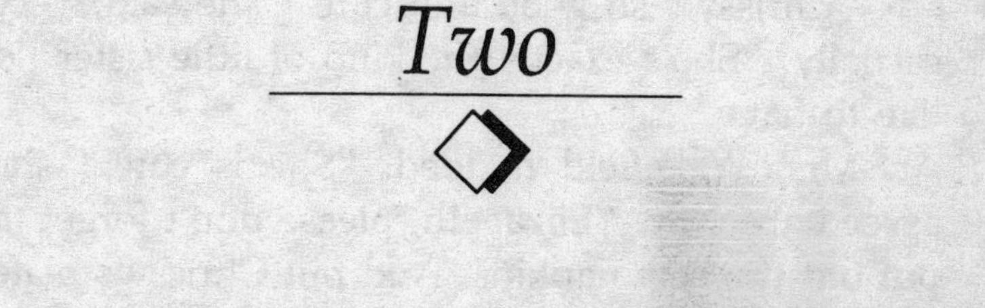

Two

"Are we having company for dinner?" Elizabeth asked as she got ready to set the table that evening.

"Yes, we are. Mr. and Mrs. Steele are coming," Mrs. Wakefield replied. "Their housekeeper is out of town, so they're bringing Chrissy, too."

Elizabeth's face brightened. "Great!" The Steeles' five-year-old daughter, Chrissy, was adorable. She had long dark braids and huge brown eyes. Elizabeth and Jessica had taken care of her for an afternoon about a year before. They'd had a terrific time swimming, blowing bubbles, and playing games.

Thinking about the fun they'd had with Chrissy reminded Elizabeth of her conversation with Jessica earlier that afternoon. She didn't always go along with her twin's schemes, but maybe this time Jessica was on to something. It would be great to have a little brother or sister. And now was a perfect time to sound out her mother on the subject.

"Chrissy's so good and cute," she said, very casually. "She's exactly the kind of little sister I'd like to have."

Mrs. Wakefield nodded. "She is cute," she agreed absently. "Elizabeth, please don't forget to put out the best napkins. And put Chrissy's plate between yours and Jessica's so you can help her with her meal."

Elizabeth sighed. It didn't sound as if her mother was very interested in having a baby. But maybe after she'd spent the evening with Chrissy she'd change her mind.

As soon as Elizabeth had finished setting the table, she ran upstairs to tell Jessica the news.

"We have to make a big fuss over Chrissy," Jessica said. "We want Mom to remember how cute little kids are."

"That won't be hard," Elizabeth said happily. "Chrissy's just like a little doll. Remember what fun we had with her? And she's so well-behaved. She didn't cry the whole time she was here."

"Leave it to me, Lizzie. Mom won't know what hit her!"

* * *

When Chrissy arrived she let out a squeal and ran toward Elizabeth and Jessica, arms out, brown eyes shining. "Jessica!" she cried. " 'Lizabeth! Let's blow bubbles!"

The twins took Chrissy into the backyard and blew bubbles and played tag. Fifteen minutes later they all came inside for dinner. "We had some bad news today," Mrs. Steele announced during the meal.

"It's really a disaster," Mr. Steele agreed. "Emily and I made reservations for a weeklong cruise, but we forgot that our housekeeper Martha's daughter is getting married that weekend and Martha will be in San Francisco for five days. That leaves no one to take care of Chrissy, so we'll have to cancel our trip."

"That's terrible!" Mrs. Wakefield said sympathetically. "But can't you take Chrissy with you?" She smiled at Chrissy, who was sitting between Elizabeth and Jessica, quietly eating her vegetables. "She's so well-behaved. I'm sure she'd be an angel."

"Unfortunately," Mr. Steele replied, "Chrissy gets seasick. She'd be miserable on a cruise." He grinned. "Anyway, she's not *always* this angelic."

"I don't like boats," Chrissy said sweetly. "Boats make me throw up." She smiled at Elizabeth. "But I like to draw boats. Can I draw a boat for you, 'Lizabeth? You can hang it in your room."

"You can draw all the boats you like after we have our dessert," Elizabeth promised.

Mrs. Steele sighed. "The cruise was going to be a second honeymoon for Alan and me," she said. "We were looking forward to being by ourselves."

Suddenly Jessica jumped up from the table. "Elizabeth and I will clear the table and get dessert."

Elizabeth stared at her twin, surprised. Jessica *never* volunteered to clear the table. Mrs. Wakefield looked surprised, too, but accepted gratefully. "Thank you, Jessica," she said.

In the kitchen, Jessica was bubbling with excitement. "I've got it, Elizabeth!" she whispered loudly.

"Got what?" Elizabeth asked, taking the ice cream from the freezer.

"An idea!" Jessica answered as she sliced the cake. "A stroke of genius! Look, the Steeles need somebody to watch Chrissy. We need to borrow a little sister or brother to prove to Mom and Dad how much help we'd be if we had a baby in the family. It's *perfect!*"

Elizabeth stared at Jessica again. She wondered if she'd heard right. "Are you suggesting that *we* keep Chrissy?"

Jessica clapped her hands. "Exactly!"

"Well, Chrissy *is* sweet," Elizabeth agreed as she spooned some ice cream on top of each piece of cake. "But it would be a lot of work, Jessica. We'd have to take her to school and pick her up and put her to bed every night and—"

"But that's why it's so perfect! It's *loads* of work. And you and I are going to do every bit of it! Mom and Dad won't have to lift a finger to help. That's what will convince them that this is the right time to have another baby." Jessica's eyes were dancing with delight. "Come on, admit it, Elizabeth. This is my grandest scheme ever."

Elizabeth put down the spoon. "Except for one small flaw."

"What's that?" Jessica asked.

Elizabeth wished she could think of a tactful way to say it, but she couldn't. "If you don't do your share of taking care of Chrissy," she said bluntly, "I'll end up with double the work."

"I promised I would, didn't I?" Jessica said shortly.

"But you've promised that about other things," Elizabeth pointed out. "And I wound up doing them for you. To tell you the truth, Jess, I'm a little tired of it."

Jessica raised her chin, her eyes flashing. "And *I'm* tired of having everybody think that you're the perfect twin and I'm the irresponsible one." She stamped her foot. "As of this moment, I am turning over a new leaf. Everybody in this family, including you, is going to see just how responsible I can be!"

Elizabeth couldn't help but be skeptical. Jessica had turned over plenty of new leaves in the past. Still, she had to agree that her twin's idea was a good one. If they *were* successful, the reward might be their own little brother or sister!

"When the Steeles leave, let's see what Mom and Dad have to say," Elizabeth suggested.

The minute the Steeles had gone home, Jessica and Elizabeth made their proposal. Mr. and Mrs. Wakefield listened carefully.

"Chrissy will need a lot of care and attention," Mrs. Wakefield cautioned. "And keeping a child for a week isn't like keeping her for an afternoon. Remember what Mr. Steele said. Chrissy isn't an angel *all* the time."

"She won't be any trouble at all," Jessica interrupted. "You can count on Elizabeth and me to do everything."

"Well, count me *out*," Steven said. "I don't mind having Chrissy around, but don't ask me to babysit!"

"We don't need you, Steven," Jessica replied haughtily. "We'll do everything ourselves."

"Are you kidding?" Steven laughed. "*Elizabeth* will wind up doing everything."

"You just wait and see," Jessica said indignantly.

Mrs. Wakefield smiled at Jessica and Elizabeth. "I think you girls have a good idea," she said. "I'm sure Mr. and Mrs. Steele will be very grateful. They might even want to pay you something for taking care of Chrissy."

"I don't think we should take any money," Jessica said quietly, and Elizabeth agreed. They were doing this good deed for other, more important reasons.

Mr. Wakefield looked impressed. "Well, I'm very proud of you two for giving Mr. and Mrs. Steele the chance to go on their second honeymoon. Of course, if you need any help with Chrissy, your mother and I will be here."

"We won't need any help," Jessica said firmly. "We're going to do it *all* ourselves."

"I'm glad to hear that you girls are willing to take on so much work," Mrs. Wakefield said gently. "And I'm sure that one little girl won't cause too much trouble. But ultimately your father and I will be responsible for her, and we're glad to do our part. We'll stay with Chrissy on Friday night while you're at the Howells' party. And if you're dead set against babysitting, Steven, why don't you take over the girls' kitchen chores while Chrissy is here?"

Mr. Wakefield grinned. "I'll help, Steven," he said, noticing the look of horror on his son's face. "We can't leave *all* the work to the girls. They'll think we're lazy bums!"

Jessica looked triumphantly at Steven, and even Elizabeth had to smile. "Then it's settled?" Elizabeth asked. "We can invite Chrissy?"

Mrs. Wakefield nodded. "I'll call the Steeles."

The Steeles were delighted with the Wakefields' offer. They arranged to drop Chrissy off on Sunday and pick her up the following Saturday.

"Let's make a schedule," Jessica suggested as she and Elizabeth went upstairs. "We can write down everything we have to do for Chrissy and decide who's going to do it."

Elizabeth looked at her sister skeptically, but Jessica appeared to be totally serious. Elizabeth raised her eyebrows. Maybe this was the first step in the right direction for the new, responsible Jessica.

In her room, Elizabeth took a sheet of paper out of her notebook and the two girls sat down on the bed. "Somebody will have to help Chrissy get dressed and braid her hair each morning. Then somebody will have to fix her breakfast," Elizabeth began.

"Somebody will have to take her to kindergarten," Jessica added thoughtfully, "and pick her up every afternoon."

"You have Booster practice on Tuesdays and ballet on Thursdays," Elizabeth reminded Jessica.

"And you've got to work on the *Sixers* on Monday and Wednesday," Jessica said. "Why don't I take charge of Chrissy on Monday and Wednesday, and you take charge of her on Tuesday and Thursday?"

"Perfect," Elizabeth agreed. "And on Friday we can split the chores. I'll take her to kindergarten and you can pick her up. That way it'll come out exactly even."

"At night we can work together," Jessica said. "We'll read her stories and get her ready for bed and things like that. This is going to be so much fun!" She picked up Elizabeth's old stuffed koala and hugged it tightly.

"We can pretend we're her big sisters," Elizabeth said.

Jessica rubbed her cheek against Elizabeth's koala. "And maybe when Mom and Dad see how responsible we are and how much help we'd be with a baby, we'll really be big sisters!"

"I can't believe you actually volunteered for a whole week of babysitting," Lila Fowler said after

Jessica had finished telling her and the other Unicorns about Chrissy's upcoming visit. It was Saturday morning, and the girls were just leaving Valley Fashions in the mall, where they'd been shopping for outfits for Janet's party.

"I don't believe it either, Jessica," Ellen Riteman said. "What a *drag*."

"No, it'll be *fun!*" Jessica protested. "It'll be just like being a big sister."

Mandy Miller laughed. "You don't know what you're in for, Jessica."

"It's mountains of work," Belinda Layton added.

Lila laughed. "Jessica's terrific when it comes to work like shopping or planning for a party. But when it comes to the *real* stuff, forget it!"

Jessica frowned. Even her *friends* thought she was irresponsible! "You guys are all wrong," she said, shaking her head. "Elizabeth and I have already planned how we're going to split up the chores. Anyway, Chrissy is a sweet little girl. It'll be a breeze."

"All kids are sweet," Mandy said wisely, "but they've all got a little devil in them, too. You should have seen my mom's face the day she found Archie fingerpainting on the kitchen wall." She grinned. "At least he had the good taste to do it in purple."

"What *I* want to know, Jessica," Ellen said, "is when you're going to see Chad Lucas again. Lila says you think he likes you."

"Chad Lucas?" Kimberly Haver sounded impressed. "The basketball player from Sweet Valley High? He's so *cute*!"

"I've seen him, too," Ellen said. "He *is* cute. But he's a high-school freshman, Jessica. He's too sophisticated to go for somebody still in middle school. You must be imagining things."

"I am not," Jessica said heatedly. "Chad and I had a terrific conversation yesterday." She conveniently left out the fact that most of the conversation had been between Chad and Steven. "What's more," she added, "he asked me if I was going to Janet's party."

When she heard that, Ellen had to admit that Jessica might not be imagining things after all. And then Lila reminded everybody that Jessica had gone out with Josh Angler, who was sixteen, *twice*.

Flirting with Josh had been exciting for Jessica. But the scheme had backfired when she wound up on a double date with her own brother. The whole thing had been too embarrassing for words. And painful! When her parents found out, she had been grounded for two entire weeks.

Mandy tossed her head. "Well," she said,

"what I want to know, Jessica, is what you are going to do about Aaron. It's not fair for you to have two cute guys when I don't even have one *ugly* one."

"I'll worry about Aaron when the time comes," Jessica said casually.

Ellen looked over Jessica's shoulder. "The time is coming right now," she said. "I mean, *Aaron's* coming. And there's a bunch of guys with him."

Jessica turned and saw Aaron approaching. *He's pretty cute, too,* she thought. *I'm going to have a hard time choosing between them.*

Suddenly a new thought struck her. *Maybe I can have them both!*

When Elizabeth got to Amy's house Saturday morning, Amy met her at the front door. She was wearing an apron and had another one in her hand.

"Hi, Elizabeth," she said, handing her the apron. "It's already after ten. We'd better get started!"

The two girls went into the kitchen and got busy. "It's a good day for the sale," Amy said happily as she took a carton of eggs out of the refrigerator. She put them on the table and turned to find the bag of chocolate chips. "No one will be home until later this—"

"Watch out!" Elizabeth cried. She made a dive for the open egg carton, which Amy had set on the very edge of the table. But she was too late. The eggs crashed to the floor, and a puddle of gooey yellow yolks spread among the broken shells.

"Yuck!" Amy groaned. "What a mess!"

"I hope you've got more," Elizabeth said. She bent down and began to pick up the broken eggshells.

"I don't," Amy replied dejectedly. "We'll have to go to the store again."

The girls hurried to the grocery store to buy another carton of eggs. "I'm getting poorer, not richer, Elizabeth!" Amy complained.

"We'll fix that," Elizabeth said, "as soon as we've sold the first batch of cookies."

But when the girls got back to the house, things didn't get much better. The first batch burned and Elizabeth dropped the second batch on the floor before they ever made it to the oven.

Amy managed a weak grin. "Well, the third batch has just *got* to turn out!"

"It better," Elizabeth agreed. She held up the almost-empty bag of chocolate chips. "We've only got enough chips for one more batch, and we wanted to start the bake sale at noon."

Amy frowned. "Only one more? But if we

charge a dime for each cookie, that means we'll only make about two dollars and fifty cents."

"Maybe we could charge fifteen cents a cookie," Elizabeth suggested. "After all, they *are* homemade."

"Good idea," Amy agreed. "That would be three seventy-five." She sighed. "That's still not as much money as I had hoped to earn, but I guess it's better than nothing."

The girls' next batch, an entire two dozen cookies, turned out beautifully. "And just in the nick of time," Amy said as she put the tray of cookies on the back porch to cool. "It's noon. Let's set up the card table on the lawn."

For the next five minutes the girls were busy setting up the card table and the sign Amy had scribbled that morning. When everything was ready they went to the back porch to get the cookies. As they rounded the back corner of the house a friendly-looking black dog with one white ear greeted them.

"He's our neighbor's new dog," Amy said as she bent down to pet him. "Hi, Cookie Monster." Cookie Monster wagged his tail.

"What a cute name for a dog," Elizabeth said as she tickled him behind his white ear.

Amy nodded. "He's called that because he

loves—" Her eyes widened and she looked at Elizabeth.

"Cookies!" Elizabeth shouted. Both girls dashed to the porch.

But they were too late. The empty tray was on the ground, and every cookie had been eaten.

"Oh, no!" Amy moaned. "What do we do now?"

Elizabeth sighed. "I guess we'll have to call off the sale."

"But we *can't*!" Amy exclaimed. "I put up signs all over the neighborhood."

"Well, we could buy some cookies," Elizabeth suggested glumly.

"I guess we have to," Amy replied.

Elizabeth and Amy raced to a bakery, where Amy spent most of the money she had left for seven dozen cookies. Then they raced back to Amy's house, put the cookies on trays, and carried them out to the card table. A few hours later, when the last cookie was sold, Amy counted what they'd taken in.

"Twelve dollars and sixty cents," she growled. "If I'm going to buy the soccer tickets for my parents, I need to raise almost twenty-two dollars in a week!" Amy exclaimed. "How am I ever going to earn that much money?"

Three

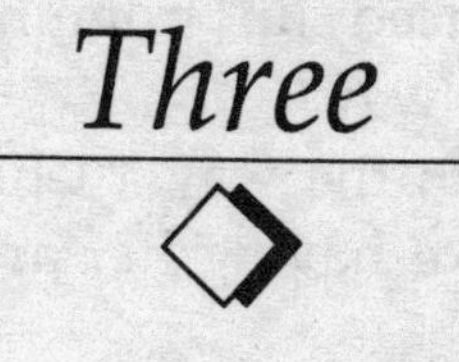

Jessica and Elizabeth spent the first part of Sunday afternoon getting ready for Chrissy's arrival. She would be sleeping on the sofa bed in the den, so the girls were cleaning up some of Steven's sports equipment that was lying around.

Jessica took Steven's gear and carried it out to the garage, where she found Chad Lucas. He and Steven were bent over their bikes.

Chad looked up from his work. "Hi, Jessica." He nodded toward some tools on the workbench. "Would you mind handing me the screwdriver?"

Jessica brought him the screwdriver and sat down beside him on the garage floor. "What are you doing?"

"I'm replacing the brake shoes on my bike," Chad said. "I'm doing it here because Steven's got the tools I need. Hand me that wrench, would you?"

Jessica handed Chad the wrench. As she did, their fingers touched. She felt a tingle and her heart thumped. Had Chad asked her for the wrench on purpose, just so he could touch her hand?

Steven glanced up from his bike. "Jessica, don't get in the way."

"She's not in the way." Chad grinned at Jessica again. "I like having her around. She's a big help."

Just then the door that led to the kitchen opened. "Jessica," Elizabeth called, "Ellen's on the phone."

Jessica scrambled to her feet. "I'm sorry," she told Chad. "I have to go."

"Too bad," Chad said. "Now I'll have to get my own tools."

Jessica hurried to the kitchen and picked up the phone. "Sorry to keep you waiting, Ellen," she said casually. "I was busy helping Chad."

There was a long pause. "Helping . . . Chad?" Ellen asked. "Helping him do what?"

"Replace the brake shoes on his bike," Jessica said, knowing that Ellen was probably dying with envy.

"He came over to *your* house to work on his bike?"

"Yeah. We had the special tools he needed," Jessica explained. "And of course," she added happily, "he wanted *me* to help. He said he likes having me around."

"He said *that?*" Ellen asked.

"That's exactly what he said," Jessica replied. "Word for word. The chemistry between us is perfect," she added dreamily. "I could feel the electricity when our fingers touched."

There was another long pause. "Well," Ellen said respectfully, "you really do have a problem, Jessica. I mean, you still like Aaron, don't you?"

"Yes, I do," Jessica groaned dramatically. "I have a *huge* problem. What am I going to do, Ellen?"

"Well, you have to do *something,*" Ellen replied firmly. "Aaron would be pretty upset if he found out about you and Chad."

At that moment Elizabeth returned to the kitchen. "Jessica, the Steeles are here," she whispered excitedly.

"I have to go now, Ellen," Jessica said.

"Well, call me back the minute you've decided what to do," Ellen instructed.

"I will," Jessica promised hastily, and hung up.

When Chrissy saw Jessica, she ran straight to

her and gave her a big hug. "Hi, Jessica!" she cried. "I've brought my swimsuit. Let's go in the pool!"

"Hang on a minute, Chrissy," Mrs. Wakefield said, laughing. "I think your parents have a few things to tell us first."

For the next few minutes, Jessica and Elizabeth listened while Mr. and Mrs. Steele gave instructions about Chrissy's kindergarten hours, bedtime, and favorite foods. Finally, Chrissy's parents kissed her good-bye and left.

"*Now* let's play in the pool," Chrissy demanded.

"OK," Elizabeth agreed, happy that Chrissy hadn't put up a fuss about her parents' leaving. "But maybe we should unpack your clothes and hang them in the closet first."

"Later," Chrissy said firmly. "I want to swim *now*."

Jessica, Elizabeth, and Chrissy changed into their swimsuits and headed for the Wakefields' backyard pool. For the next half-hour, they swam, played, and chased Chrissy around the pool.

"I'm done swimming," Chrissy finally announced. The girls went indoors to change, and the twins helped Chrissy unpack. Afterward, the girls helped Mrs. Wakefield make fudge.

When the last batch of fudge was done, Jessica couldn't help but smile. Chrissy had chocolate smeared on her face and hands. She was a mess, but a *cute* mess. "Come on, Chrissy," she said, holding out her hand, "let's go wash up."

"No! I want a piece first," Chrissy cried, dashing to the table.

"Not now," Elizabeth said gently. "It has to cool first."

"*Now*," Chrissy said decidedly. She touched the fudge and the soft, gooey chocolate stuck to her hand. "Yucky," she said, making a sour face.

"Fudge has to get hard before you can eat it," Elizabeth explained as she wiped Chrissy's hands. "You have to be patient."

Chrissy looked as if she were going to cry, and Jessica felt sorry for her. "Would you like to look at some pretty fish while you wait for the candy to cool, Chrissy?"

Chrissy brightened. "Fish are my favorite animal."

Mr. and Mrs. Howard, who lived next door, had a large aquarium in their family room.

"So this is Chrissy," Mrs. Howard said when she came to the back door. "We've heard a lot about you. Are you having fun with the twins, Chrissy?"

But Chrissy didn't answer. She ran straight to the aquarium, which held several brightly colored tropical fish, a pink ceramic castle for the fish to swim through, and delicate branches of bright green water plants.

"Zebras!" Chrissy squealed as she pressed her nose against the glass. "Look, 'Lizabeth, they're all stripey!"

"Those are zebra*fish*, honey," Mrs. Howard explained to Chrissy as she settled herself in front of the aquarium. But Chrissy lost interest in the fish after only five minutes.

"What do we do now?" Chrissy asked.

Jessica and Elizabeth exchanged glances. They both realized that it was going to take a lot of energy to keep up with Chrissy.

"Here are your pajamas, Chrissy," Jessica said, handing her a pair of pink ones.

Chrissy shook her head. "I want to wear my blue jammies," she said emphatically.

"I don't see any blue ones," Elizabeth said, looking through Chrissy's clothing. "You'll have to wear the pink ones."

"But I don't *want* pink," Chrissy said. "I want the blue ones!" Her big brown eyes filled with tears. "I can't go to sleep without my blue jammies!"

Jessica put her arm around Chrissy. "How

would you like to sleep in my blue T-shirt?" she whispered. "It has a panda on the front."

Chrissy stopped crying. "Maybe," she said cautiously.

Jessica's panda T-shirt came down to Chrissy's knees, but Chrissy loved it. "This is better than my blue jammies, Jessica," she said happily. Then she brushed her teeth and snuggled into Jessica's lap while Jessica read *The Cat That Wouldn't Behave.* Afterward, Elizabeth sang "Puff the Magic Dragon," and the twins tucked Chrissy into bed and kissed her good night.

"I don't know about you," Jessica said wearily when she and Elizabeth had gone upstairs, "but I'm pooped! She wears me out."

"Me, too," Elizabeth agreed. The twins were both on Elizabeth's bed when Mrs. Wakefield came in. "I want to compliment you girls on your work with Chrissy today," she said proudly. "You're doing a great job."

"Thanks, Mom," Jessica said. It was nice to be complimented for being responsible, for a change. "I just wish Chrissy was going to be here longer than a week," she added, with a meaningful glance at Elizabeth. "Being a big sister is terrific."

Elizabeth immediately got the hint. "It's great

to have a little sister to take care of, especially one like Chrissy."

Mrs. Wakefield smiled. "I'm glad you're enjoying it," she said. "But by the end of the week you'll probably be glad to have Chrissy go back home."

"Oh, no, Mom," Jessica protested. "As far as we're concerned, she can stay *forever!*"

"Well, we'll see," Mrs. Wakefield replied. "I reserve the right to say 'I told you so.' " She smiled as she kissed them each goodnight and left.

"I haven't even had a chance to tell you my news, Lizzie! Wait till you hear." Jessica smiled proudly. "Would you believe it if I told you that Chad Lucas *likes* me?"

Elizabeth frowned. "To tell you the truth, no," she said. "I wouldn't believe it."

"Well, he *does,*" Jessica insisted. "He told Steven on Friday that it was nice to have a cute girl to get him things. Today he let me hand him his tools and he told Steven that he liked having me around. He said I was a big help."

Elizabeth eyed Jessica skeptically. "Maybe Chad just likes having you *do* things for him."

"Don't be silly, Elizabeth," Jessica said scornfully. "Chad isn't that kind of person. He likes me for *myself*. But now I've got a huge problem. What do I do about Aaron?"

"If you're not fooling yourself," Elizabeth said slowly, "your big problem is what to do about *Chad*. Remember Josh Angler? Mom and Dad would pop their corks if they found out that you were involved with *another* older guy!"

Jessica shuddered. She hated thinking about what had happened with Josh. "Don't remind me, Elizabeth. It was the most embarrassing thing that's ever happened to me."

"Then you'd better forget Chad," Elizabeth advised.

Jessica hated to admit it, but Elizabeth was probably right. Even if she wanted to, though, she couldn't make Chad stop liking her, could she? She couldn't make Aaron stop liking her, either. It was awful, Jessica thought, but at the same time it was incredibly flattering. How many other girls were torn between two cute boys?

Jessica was scheduled to take care of Chrissy on Monday morning. Elizabeth woke her up. "Jessica, you're going to be late. Don't forget Chrissy."

"Chrissy!" Jessica exclaimed, sitting bolt upright. She jumped out of bed and hurried into her clothes.

Chrissy was still asleep, the blanket pulled up to her chin. Jessica felt a wave of tenderness wash over her when she saw the tousled head on the pillow. "Wake up, Chrissy," she said gently. "It's time for school."

"No," Chrissy said sleepily as she pulled the blanket higher. It took Jessica a full five minutes to persuade Chrissy to get out of bed and get dressed. Then Chrissy put up a fuss about having her hair brushed and braided.

"You're hurting!" she cried when Jessica tried to get the brush through the tangles. "I hate getting my hair braided."

"I'm sorry, Chrissy," Jessica said quickly. "But I have to do it."

"You don't do it as good as Martha. I want Martha. I want my mother, too." Her little chin quivered. "I want to go home."

"I know," Jessica said softly. She'd have cried, too, if she'd been five years old and away from home for the first time. "What color ribbons do you want to wear with your red-and-yellow outfit?" she asked.

"I don't want to wear any ribbons," Chrissy said. She pouted. But a minute later she changed her mind. "I'll wear the yellow ones," she decided. Then, just as Jessica got them tied properly, she changed her mind again. "I want red," she said. By the time Chrissy was finally dressed, Jessica was ready to go back to bed!

Mr. Wakefield was just finishing his coffee when Jessica and Chrissy came into the kitchen. "I like your red ribbons, Chrissy." He picked up his briefcase and gave both girls a hug. "Have a good day," he said as he left.

Jessica poured cereal into a bowl. "I don't like cornflakes," Chrissy objected. "Martha gives me cereal that comes with sugar."

"Sugar-coated cereal isn't good for you," Jessica said firmly. She reached for a box of wheat flakes, but Chrissy didn't want those either.

"I'll have peanut butter and toast," Chrissy decided at last. After Jessica had prepared Chrissy's breakfast, she had just enough time to wolf down a bowl of cereal before it was time to leave for their walk to the kindergarten.

Halfway to the school, Chrissy started to drag her feet. Jessica took her by the hand and pulled her along. "Martha always drives me in the car," she complained. "I want Martha to drive me."

"Martha can't drive you," Jessica said, trying to be patient. She gave Chrissy's hand a tug. "Come on, Chrissy. You have to walk faster, or we'll both be late."

Chrissy burst into tears and yanked her hand away. "You're hurting me!" she cried. "You're mean, Jessica!"

During this commotion, Jessica spied Bruce Patman turning the corner. Bruce was the last person in the world she wanted to see right then.

"Well, if it isn't Jessica," Bruce drawled. He glanced down at Chrissy. "What's wrong, kid?"

Now that she had an audience, Chrissy really turned on the tears. "She's hurting me!" she wailed. "She pulled my hand and made me run."

Bruce grinned at Jessica. "If you ask me, the kid's a brat. She needs somebody to show her who's boss." Hearing Bruce's words, Chrissy began to cry louder.

Even though Chrissy was being a real pain, Jessica still liked her. What's more, she was responsible for Chrissy. And nobody, not even the cutest and most popular boy in seventh grade, was going to get away with a bullying remark like that.

Jessica put her hands on her hips. "She is *not* a brat," she said heatedly. "She's a little upset this morning, that's all. She's homesick."

Bruce shrugged. "OK," he said. "If you want

to be stuck with a bawling kid, it's your problem." He sauntered off down the street.

There was a silence. Then Chrissy reached up and took Jessica's hand. "Let's hurry," she said. "I don't want to miss show and tell."

Jessica laughed affectionately at Chrissy's change of mood. "Sure," she said. "Let's hurry."

When Jessica went to pick up Chrissy at kindergarten that afternoon, she was relieved that Chrissy behaved so well. She was *so* relieved that she took Chrissy to the park to play on the merry-go-round. After that, they went for a visit to the Howards' to say hello to the fish. They wound up the afternoon by watching *Sesame Street* and having a snack.

At dinner that evening, Chrissy excitedly told everybody about her day. "Me and Jessica had so much fun."

"And what about you, Jessica?" Mrs. Wakefield asked. "Did you have a good time, too?"

Jessica didn't know what to say. Merry-go-rounds and *Sesame Street* might have been OK when she was five years old. But she was twelve now, and there was only one word to describe the afternoon she'd spent with Chrissy.

That word was *boring!*

Four

On Monday afternoon, Amy hurried home from school and got the lawn mower out of her garage. She had decided that the fastest way to earn money was to mow lawns. It was hard work, but she still had a lot of money to earn. If she charged five dollars per job and got five jobs by Saturday, she could buy the soccer tickets for her parents. Amy didn't have much experience with yard work, but at this point she didn't have much of a choice. She could never collect enough cans, she was out of the cookie business for good, and she just hadn't been able to think of any other way to earn money in such a short period of time.

Pushing the mower with one hand and carrying hedge clippers and a rake awkwardly in the other, Amy started down the block. Her intention was to knock on every door and ask if the residents wanted their lawns mowed.

At the third house, Mrs. Anderson was interested. "The grass does need cutting," she agreed. "But I'm very particular about my lawn and shrubbery. Do you think you can do a good job?"

"I'll do my best," Amy vowed.

Mrs. Anderson showed Amy all the things she wanted done and then she headed toward her car. "I've got to run an errand, so I won't be here to supervise you." She eyed Amy doubtfully. "Are you sure you can handle this work?"

Amy was sorry she had found such a demanding first customer, but it was too late to back out. "I'm sure I can manage," she replied as confidently as she could.

"And be sure *not* to touch those plants," Mrs. Anderson added, walking around the side of the house. She pointed to two tropical-looking plants just beyond the hedge at the corner of the house. "They're very rare."

The afternoon was warm and long. When Amy finally finished cutting, raking, and bagging the grass, she hurried to clip the hedges. It was almost five o'clock, and she had to be home for dinner by five-thirty.

Amy began to clip off unruly branches as fast as she could. Finally she turned the corner of the house. She took two more big snips and then stopped, her eyes widening in horror. The plant she had just lopped the top off of was one of the rare tropical plants Mrs. Anderson had told her not to touch!

For a second Amy panicked. *Maybe I can stuff the cut-off branches into a sack with the hedge clippings, and Mrs. Anderson might not notice right away!* Then she shook her head. That wasn't fair, and it wasn't honest. She'd have to confess that she had snipped the head off the rare plant and offer to pay for it.

Mrs. Anderson got back from her errands just as Amy was finishing up. "You've done a pretty good job," she said critically as she surveyed the yard, "although that hedge isn't very straight at the corner."

Amy drew in her breath. "I have to show you something," she said. She led Mrs. Anderson around the corner of the house.

"You've killed my plant!" Mrs. Anderson cried.

"I'm sorry," Amy said, hanging her head. "It was an accident."

Mrs. Anderson scowled at Amy. "That plant was worth a lot of money."

"I'll pay for it," Amy said. "If I can," she added miserably. "I don't have much money."

For a minute Mrs. Anderson was silent. She looked around the yard at all the work Amy had done. "I'll pay you two dollars for everything you've done, instead of the amount we first agreed upon," she said finally. "Do you think that's fair?"

"I guess," Amy said glumly. She could see that Mrs. Anderson's offer was fair, but somehow it didn't seem *right.* She had worked all afternoon in the heat and had earned only two dollars. She still had to find a way to earn some money—and fast!

Chrissy had behaved herself all through dinner that Monday evening. But afterward, when the twins sat down to do their homework, she pestered them to play a board game she'd brought with her from home. Finally, feeling responsible, the twins put their homework aside and played Chutes and Ladders until eight o'clock, Chrissy's bedtime.

"That's got to be the most boring game ever invented," Jessica grumbled to Elizabeth as they were helping Chrissy brush her teeth.

"It is *not* boring!" Chrissy said heatedly.

Jessica immediately felt ashamed of herself. "You're right, Chrissy," she said apologetically. "I used the wrong word. I should have said it was *fun.*"

Elizabeth glanced at the clock in the den as they kissed Chrissy goodnight and tucked her into bed. "Eight o'clock. Time to watch that mystery I've been looking forward to."

Then Jessica and Elizabeth looked at each other. It had just dawned on them that the television was there in the den, where Chrissy was sleeping.

"I guess I'll have to skip the mystery," Elizabeth said, sounding disappointed.

"That's OK," Jessica said. "We can listen to my new Melody Powers tape."

As the twins headed back upstairs, Elizabeth said, "Maybe we should add a few rules to our Chrissy schedule. After all, being responsible for her means *not* doing some things, as well as doing others."

Jessica frowned. Being responsible was getting very complicated. But she agreed with Elizabeth. Now that there was a little child in the house, there were some things they wouldn't be able to do. So the twins went into Jessica's room, turned on the stereo, and made a new list. Number one on the list was the new rule: no TV after eight o'clock.

"That means I won't get to watch the show I wanted to watch Wednesday night, either," Jessica complained. "I wonder if Belinda Layton had to give up TV when her brother was born?"

"It's only because Chrissy's sleeping in the den," Elizabeth reminded her. "If we had a new baby, he or she wouldn't sleep there."

Jessica looked closely at Elizabeth. She had just thought of something awful. "Just where *would* the baby sleep?" she asked.

Elizabeth frowned. "I guess one of us would have to give up her room."

"No *way*," Jessica said firmly, shaking her head. "I waited a long time to have my own room. I'm not giving it up for anybody, not even a new baby!"

"Jessica," Mr. Wakefield said as he stuck his head inside, "your music woke Chrissy up. Please turn it down. And see if you can get her back to sleep. OK?"

"OK," Jessica sighed. "Better add something else to the Chrissy schedule, Elizabeth. Number two: don't play music after Chrissy's in bed."

"There's a number three, too," Elizabeth said as she scribbled. "Whoever wakes up Chrissy has to read her back to sleep."

"I guess that's me," Jessica sighed. "I'm the one who turned the volume so high." She turned off the music and headed downstairs.

"I can't believe how responsible you're being, Jessica," Elizabeth called after her.

"Neither can I," Jessica admitted. "I guess it comes from being a big sister." She grinned.

"Maybe I'll even close up that four-minute gap between the two of us!"

In the den, Jessica settled down to read *The Cat That Wouldn't Behave,* which, in her opinion, was very dull. But Chrissy loved it and snuggled up close to listen. Jessica only had to read the story four times before her "little sister" finally fell asleep.

On Tuesday it was Elizabeth's turn to take care of Chrissy.

"I can't go to kindergarten," Chrissy said when Elizabeth went to the den to get her up. "I've got a sore throat."

Elizabeth looked in Chrissy's mouth. "It doesn't look red. I think you'll be OK."

Then Chrissy gave a phony-sounding cough. "But I've got a cold, too," she said. "Martha lets me stay home and play with her when I'm sick."

Elizabeth nodded. She was beginning to understand. Chrissy was pretending to be sick because she wanted attention. "If your cough gets worse," she said comfortingly, "you can have some cough medicine. It tastes yucky, but it'll make you better."

"I'm better," Chrissy decided, scrambling out of bed. She shook her head at the green shirt Elizabeth pulled out of the closet. "I want to wear my yellow shirt with the ballerina on it," she said.

"All the kids wear their ballerina shirts on Tuesdays because we have dance."

Elizabeth searched through all of the clothes Chrissy had brought with her, but she couldn't find the shirt. "I guess your mommy and daddy didn't pack it," she said finally.

"I can't go to school without my ballerina shirt," Chrissy wailed. "I want Martha! I want to go home!"

Elizabeth put her arms around the little girl and pulled her close. "It's tough to be on your own and away from home," she said gently. "But I know you're grown-up enough to handle it."

"I'm grown-up?" Chrissy asked. She sounded surprised. "But Martha always says I'm her baby. That's why I get to stay home when I don't feel like going to school."

"Well, Jessica and I think you're *very* grown-up," Elizabeth said. "Your mom and dad must think so, too, or they wouldn't have let you stay with us."

Chrissy looked thoughtful for a minute. Then she said, "I think I'll have cornflakes for breakfast."

When the girls were on their way to the kindergarten, Chrissy broke out crying when she saw one of her classmates wearing a ballerina shirt.

"I want my shirt!" she shrieked. "I can't dance without my shirt!"

Firmly, Elizabeth reached for Chrissy's hand. "I understand that you're upset, Chrissy," she said. "But if we don't hurry, we're both going to be late." Just then, Elizabeth looked up to see Bruce Patman approaching. Jessica and the Unicorns might think that Bruce was cute, but in Elizabeth's opinion he was a conceited snob.

"If it isn't the brat again," Bruce said. He glanced at Elizabeth. "I told your sister yesterday, that kid needs somebody to show her who's boss."

Chrissy stopped crying and stared up at Bruce. Then, without warning, she kicked him in the shin, hard.

"Ow!" Bruce exclaimed, grabbing his leg. "Elizabeth, that bratty little kid *kicked* me!"

Elizabeth tried not to smile, but secretly her heart was dancing a jig. "I guess she just wanted to show *you* who's boss," she said with a straight face. "Chrissy, it's not nice to kick people. Apologize to Bruce."

"I know it's not nice to kick." Chrissy glared at Bruce. "But it's not nice to call people brats, either. He can 'pologize to *me* first."

Without another word, Elizabeth abruptly took Chrissy's hand and walked away from Bruce as fast as she could. She was about to burst into laughter. She couldn't tell Chrissy that she was proud of her for having stood up to a bully, because of the way she did it. But when Elizabeth left Chrissy at the kindergarten, she gave her an extra hug and kiss.

Elizabeth was still smiling over what had happened when she got to school. While she was getting her books out of her locker, Todd Wilkins came along. Some of the kids at school thought Todd was Elizabeth's boyfriend because they had been at a bowling party together and because they sometimes ate lunch together. Elizabeth wasn't sure how she felt about being called Todd's girlfriend, but she liked Todd in a special way. They hadn't talked much lately because she'd been busy with the *Sixers* and Todd had basketball practice nearly every afternoon.

"Hi, Elizabeth," Todd said. "What are you smiling about?"

When Elizabeth told him about Chrissy and Bruce Patman, Todd chuckled, too. They were still laughing when Amy came along a minute later. "I'm glad *you* guys have something to laugh about," she said glumly.

"What's wrong, Amy?" Elizabeth asked.

"Yesterday I got a job mowing a lawn for five dollars. But I had to settle for only two dollars."

"Two dollars?" Todd asked. "*Any* lawn is worth more than that. What happened?"

Amy frowned. "I lopped off the top of some stupid tropical plant. The woman said it was worth a lot of money, so she only paid me two dollars for all my hard work. I'm out of the lawn-mowing business for good. And I've still got a lot of money to earn by the end of the week. Can you guys think of anything? I'm desperate."

"I've got an idea," Todd offered. "My cousin set up a garage-cleaning service and he made a ton of money."

Amy looked interested. "No chance of killing any rare plants, either," she said. "It sounds like a foolproof business."

"Just don't hire yourself out for Friday night," Elizabeth said. "Remember, that's the night of Janet's party."

"How could I forget?" Amy asked. "Everybody's talking about it."

"Are you going?" Todd asked Elizabeth.

Elizabeth nodded. "Are you?"

"Sure," Todd replied enthusiastically. "I hear that Joe has a terrific model railroad set up in his basement. I've been wanting to see it. Maybe we'll have time to talk, too." Todd waved goodbye and walked off.

Elizabeth smiled happily to herself. She was

looking forward to Janet's party more than she'd looked forward to anything for a long time. It would be great to spend part of the evening with Todd.

"Hey, Elizabeth," Amy said, "I've got an idea. How about if we went into the garage-cleaning business together? I'll bet two would make more money than one, and the work would be more fun, too."

Elizabeth smiled. "Sorry, Amy, but I've already got a job this week. I have to take care of Chrissy, remember?"

"Oh, yeah," Amy said. "How's it going?"

Just then, Jessica interrupted. "It's *tough,*" she said, walking up behind them.

"Chrissy isn't exactly the angel we thought she was," Elizabeth agreed. "Maybe the trouble is that we expected her to act like someone our age, instead of like a five-year-old."

"A five-year-old?" Jessica laughed. "Most of the time she acts like a *three*-year-old."

"Maybe," Elizabeth said. "But I have to admire her spirit. Bruce Patman tried to bully her this morning and she kicked him."

"Kicked Bruce Patman!" Jessica repeated, awestruck.

Amy laughed. "Well, if you ask me, some little kids are a lot smarter than people give them credit for."

Five

Tuesday afternoon after school, Elizabeth went to Chrissy's kindergarten to pick her up. Chrissy was coloring a picture, but the minute she saw Elizabeth she pushed her crayons away. "I want to go to the park!" she announced.

"We can go for a little while," Elizabeth replied, smiling at Chrissy's eagerness. "But it looks like rain, so we may not be able to stay. We can get an ice-cream cone, though," she added. "Would you like that?"

Chrissy nodded and took Elizabeth's hand. "Will there be any big boys at the park?" she asked cautiously.

Elizabeth laughed, remembering Chrissy's encounter with Bruce Patman. "If there are, they'd better watch out for *you,*" she said. "But if you're thinking of the boy you met this morning, he's not likely to be there."

"Good," Chrissy said. "I don't like big boys. They're bossy." She paused, considering. "Except for Steven. He's nice. He listens to me." Chrissy took two skipping steps. "Can you skip?" she asked Elizabeth.

"You bet I can! Watch this!" Elizabeth was a little out of practice, but she managed to skip all the way to the park beside Chrissy.

When they got to the park Chrissy ran straight for the merry-go-round. Elizabeth pushed her around and around until she was out of breath. "That's it for the merry-go-round, Chrissy," she said at last. "I'm pooped!"

Without protest, Chrissy jumped off the ride and ran for the swings. "Push me high, 'Liza-beth," she shrieked, and Elizabeth pushed with all her might. Then Chrissy jumped off the swing and ran to the slide, where she climbed to the top and slid all the way down on her stomach.

"You're not supposed to go down on your stomach," Elizabeth said when Chrissy had landed. She pointed to a sign on the slide. "It's against park rules."

Chrissy tossed her head defiantly and climbed the ladder again. "You can't stop me," she yelled from the top of the slide, and started down on her stomach again.

"Hi, Elizabeth," Todd Wilkins said as he pulled up beside her on his bicycle.

Elizabeth smiled back, glad for this unexpected chance to talk to him. "I thought you had basketball practice today," she said.

"I did," Todd replied. "But I had to leave early to go somewhere with my parents. I was passing the park on my way home when I saw you." He squinted up at Chrissy, who was climbing back up the ladder once more. "That's Chrissy, huh?"

"Look at me, 'Lizabeth!" Chrissy yelled, starting down headfirst for the third time. Chrissy slid down too fast and flew into the sandpile at the foot of the slide. When she scrambled up, she was screaming at the top of her lungs. Elizabeth rushed to her, with Todd close behind.

"Are you all right?" Elizabeth asked anxiously.

"I've got sand in my mouth," Chrissy sputtered. "My elbow's broken, and my braid is all loose."

Elizabeth knelt down and gathered the little girl into her arms. "It's OK, Chrissy," she crooned. Then she looked at Chrissy's elbow. "Your elbow's only scraped. When we get home, we'll find a Band-Aid for it." She began to fix Chrissy's loose braid.

Chrissy glanced up. "Who's that big boy?" she asked suspiciously, pointing at Todd.

"That's Todd Wilkins," Elizabeth said, dusting Chrissy off. "He's very nice," she added hastily. For all she knew, Chrissy liked to kick *all* big boys, not just obnoxious ones such as Bruce Patman. "He's not bossy at all."

"Hi, Chrissy," Todd said with an amused grin.

Chrissy forgot about her scraped elbow. "Is Elizabeth your girlfriend?" she asked.

Elizabeth drew a sharp breath. What a horrible question to ask! "Chrissy," she said helplessly, "it's not polite to ask personal questions."

Chrissy didn't pay any attention to Elizabeth. " 'Lizabeth says you're nice and not bossy," she told Todd, "so she must be your girlfriend." She smiled. "Are you her boyfriend?"

Todd looked down at his sneakers. "Just because somebody thinks you're nice doesn't necessarily mean she's your girlfriend," he muttered, the red rising in his cheeks. He darted Elizabeth an uncomfortable look. Chrissy had definitely put him on the spot!

At that moment there was a loud clap of

thunder that made all three of them jump. A few fat raindrops splattered on the grass. Todd got on his bike. "I'd better get home before it pours," he said. "See you tomorrow, Elizabeth."

"I think you're 'Lizabeth's boyfriend," Chrissy yelled at the top of her lungs, but Todd didn't look back.

Elizabeth looked around nervously. What if somebody from school had heard Chrissy yelling? But there was no one else around, only the ice-cream truck parked at the edge of the grass. She was safe, at least for now. "Come on, Chrissy," she said hurriedly. "Let's go home before we get wet."

Chrissy pointed to the ice-cream truck. "But you promised me some ice cream."

"The ice-cream man is closing his truck," Elizabeth said. "See? He's putting up his shutters because of the rain."

"I want ice cream!" Chrissy screamed and folded her arms. "You promised me ice cream, 'Lizabeth!"

"There *isn't* any ice cream!" Elizabeth said. It was raining harder now. "Come on, Chrissy. You're getting wet. We're *both* getting wet."

"I don't care! I'm not going anywhere until I get my ice cream!"

The ice-cream man looked in their direction.

"If she'll settle for an ice-cream bar," he called to Elizabeth, "I can fix you up."

Clutching the ice-cream bar Elizabeth bought her, Chrissy hurried to keep up as they walked quickly through the rain. Elizabeth wanted to begin some important schoolwork when they got home, but Chrissy begged to see the Howards' tropical fish. Once they were at the Howards' she only wanted to stay a few minutes. Did all little sisters behave this way, Elizabeth wondered, or did Chrissy have a special stubborn streak?

After Elizabeth finally talked Chrissy into watching *Sesame Street,* she went in to help her mother with dinner and to ask for some advice. "I'm beginning to think Chrissy's really spoiled," she said. "What do you think, Mom?"

Mrs. Wakefield nodded. "When a child always gets what she wants, that's what she learns to expect."

Chrissy came into the kitchen. " 'Lizabeth's got a boyfriend," she announced, taking an orange off the table.

Elizabeth sucked in her breath. *What next?*

"That's interesting," Mrs. Wakefield said mildly. She smiled at Elizabeth and took the orange away from Chrissy. "Dinner's almost ready."

Elizabeth gave her mother a grateful look.

Chrissy reached for the orange again and glanced at Elizabeth. "His name is Todd," she said.

"That's a nice name," Mrs. Wakefield replied. She took the orange and handed Chrissy some silverware. "Let's see if you're grown-up enough to help Elizabeth set the table."

Occupied with setting the table, Chrissy seemed to forget about Todd. But Elizabeth suddenly felt nervous. It wasn't so bad for Chrissy to talk about Todd to Mrs. Wakefield, but what if she came out with something like that in front of Steven? He'd never let Elizabeth hear the end of it!

Jessica spent Tuesday afternoon with the Boosters, the cheering and baton squad the Unicorns had organized. With the exception of Amy Sutton, all eight Boosters were Unicorns. Amy wasn't at practice that day, though. She'd told Jessica she had something very important to do, and that she'd make up the practice later. The rest of the Boosters were in the gym learning the new cheers. The boys' basketball team was there, too, including Aaron Dallas, Jake Hamilton, and Rick Hunter. The Boosters, especially Jessica, Lila, and Ellen, spent as much time flirting with the boys as they did practicing cheers.

During a time-out, Aaron stopped beside Jessica. "I'd like to walk you home after practice," he said, "but I've got something to do."

Jessica smiled happily. Having Aaron say he'd *like* to walk her home was almost as good as having him do it.

"You're going to Janet's party Friday night, aren't you?" Aaron went on. "Maybe we can get together then."

Jessica nodded, hoping that Ellen was listening. "Yes, I'm going," she said. "It'll be a great party."

"Joe's got a neat model railroad, too, I hear. See you there." Aaron waved and went back to the game.

After practice, Jessica walked home with Ellen. Ellen admitted that she had been listening, and she was obviously impressed by what Aaron had said. Suddenly Ellen clutched Jessica's arm. "Jessica," she hissed, "that's Chad Lucas over there on that bike!"

Jessica looked over and nodded very casually, even though her heart was beginning to pound.

Ellen gasped. "He is *so* cute!"

Chad rode toward them, then stopped and

leaned on the handlebars. "Hi, Jessica. Have you seen Steven around this afternoon?"

Jessica shook her head and looked down at Chad's bike. "I see your brakes are working perfectly."

"Thanks to you," Chad said. He smiled at Ellen. "Jessica is the world's champion tool-getter."

Jessica smiled as Ellen gave her a respectful glance. She couldn't *believe* this was happening. Chad Lucas was saying such incredibly wonderful things about her in front of her friend! It just proved that she had been right from the beginning. Chad definitely had a crush on her.

"Well," Chad said, "I guess I'll see you later."

"At the party Friday night," Jessica reminded him, carelessly tossing her head.

"Oh, yeah." He grinned. "Hey, maybe we can dance together, huh?" Waving, he sped off.

Ellen let out her breath with a rush. "Jessica!" she squealed. "Chad Lucas practically asked you for a date!"

"I wouldn't say that," Jessica said modestly. "He just said we'd dance together at the party."

"Well, that's as good as a date," Ellen replied. "He really *does* like you."

Jessica nodded. "I think he does," she agreed happily. In fact, she was *sure* of it.

Ellen's excitement faded. "But what are you going to do about Aaron? He's expecting you to be with him at the party. I heard him say so."

But Jessica hadn't heard her question. She had momentarily lapsed into her own little dream world. *Two* boys struggling for her attention—it was too much!

"Jessica," Ellen repeated anxiously. "What are you going to do?"

"I've decided to give Chad up," Jessica said abruptly. The moment the words came out of her mouth, she knew she was doing the decent thing. Chad was cuter than Aaron, and he was a basketball star, but he was at least two years older than she was, which was definitely a problem. Especially after what had happened with Josh Angler. Aaron was definitely a much safer person to have as a boyfriend.

"You're giving Chad up?" Ellen cried. She clasped her hands. "Oh, Jessica, how *romantic!*"

"Yes," Jessica said, gratified by Ellen's response. "I know that Chad will be terribly unhappy when he hears that there's no future for us. But he'll have to learn to live without me." She put an extra quiver into her voice. "I'd rather *perish* than hurt Aaron."

Ellen looked awed. "When are you going to tell Chad?"

"Soon," Jessica said evasively. Now that she thought about it, she didn't much like the idea of actually *telling* Chad she was rejecting him. It would be embarrassing for both of them. Maybe if she just dropped out of his life, he'd get the hint.

They came to the Wakefields' street and Jessica said goodbye to Ellen. "As soon as you've told Chad you're giving him up, call me," Ellen pressed. "I want to know how he takes it."

"I will," Jessica promised, and headed for home with a smile on her face. She was really enjoying the idea of having two boys breaking their hearts over her. What more could a girl want?

The first three people Amy approached Tuesday after school said that they didn't need their garages cleaned and Amy was about to give up. But the fourth, Mr. Andretti, a grandfatherly man with gray hair and a cane, was glad to hire her.

"It's a big job," Mr. Andretti said, shaking his head. "I've got so much stuff in the garage, I can't even get my car in there anymore. Are you sure you want the job?"

"I'm sure," Amy said. Actually, she didn't want the job, she wanted the *money*. But she couldn't have one without the other.

When Mr. Andretti opened the garage door

for her, though, Amy was startled. The garage was absolutely stuffed. First Amy had to move everything out into the driveway and then sweep the garage floor. Then, while Mr. Andretti sorted out the things he wanted to keep, Amy hauled boxes of trash out to the curb. When that was done, she put all that remained onto shelves, hung up the garden tools, and tied a big pile of old newspapers into bundles. When she finally finished, she was dead tired and dripping with sweat.

"That was a lot of work for six dollars," Mr. Andretti said from his rocking chair on the porch, where he'd sat down to oversee the last part of the job.

Amy dropped down on the porch steps. "Yes, it was," she said wearily, looking at her scratched, dirty hands. Cleaning out garages was even more work than mowing lawns! But Amy felt a little better when Mr. Andretti handed her the six dollars plus a fifty-cent tip. All she had left to earn now was about fourteen dollars. Only three more jobs and she'd have more than enough money for the soccer tickets!

"While you were busy with those newspapers, I talked to my daughter. She lives just down the street," Mr. Andretti said. "She'd like to have you clean out her garage on Thursday afternoon. How does that sound?"

The thought of cleaning another garage made her want to scream. Instead, she straightened her shoulders.

"It sounds great. If you'll give me her address, I'll be there Thursday afternoon." With Thursday's job, one on Friday, and another on Saturday, she'd be able to buy the tickets!

Six

The twins found that getting Chrissy to sleep wasn't any easier on Tuesday night than it had been on Monday. After several interminable games of Chutes and Ladders, Chrissy finally agreed to take a bath, brush her teeth, and put on Jessica's panda T-shirt. "I'm ready for my favorite story, 'Lizabeth," she said sweetly as she climbed into her bed in the den. She gave Jessica an angelic smile. "Sing me my favorite song, too," she commanded. Elizabeth read *The Cat That Wouldn't Behave* three times, and Jessica sang "Puff the Magic Dragon" twice. Finally, Chrissy fell asleep, and the twins tiptoed out of the den.

"Whew," Jessica whispered as she shut the door behind them. "I thought she'd *never* go to sleep."

Elizabeth nodded. "Don't forget the rules we wrote down last night."

"No TV," Jessica sighed regretfully as they went up the stairs.

"No loud music, either," Elizabeth said. At that moment the phone began to ring. Elizabeth ran to the kitchen and picked up the receiver. It was Julie Porter, one of Elizabeth's friends on the *Sixers* staff.

A couple of minutes later, Elizabeth was so deep in her conversation with Julie that she didn't see Chrissy pad barefoot across the floor to the refrigerator. She didn't even know that Chrissy was in the room until the little girl opened the refrigerator door and took out a carton of orange juice.

"What are you doing up?" Elizabeth asked, startled. "You're supposed to be asleep!"

"What did you say, Elizabeth?" Julie asked.

"I *was* asleep," Chrissy replied accusingly. "The telephone woke me up. Now I'm thirsty." She gave Elizabeth a curious look. "Are you talking to your boyfriend?"

"He *isn't* my boyfriend," Elizabeth said firmly.

"*Who* isn't your boyfriend?" Julie asked, sounding confused. "What are you talking about, Elizabeth?"

"Todd," Elizabeth said into the phone. She shook her head at Chrissy. "Be careful with that orange-juice carton, Chrissy. It's too heavy for you."

"Todd," Chrissy repeated, still holding the carton. She did a little dance. " 'Lizabeth's talking to Todd," she sang delightedly. " 'Lizabeth's talking to Todd."

"I am *not* talking to Todd!" Elizabeth said. "Put that juice back, Chrissy!"

"Elizabeth," Julie said, "would you like to call me back later, after you've taken care of whatever it is you have to do?"

"Thanks, Julie," Elizabeth said. "Talk to you later." She hung up the phone. "Chrissy, give me that orange juice before you spill—"

Thud! went the orange-juice carton.

"Oh, no," Elizabeth moaned, covering her face with her hands as orange juice splashed all over the floor.

"My panda shirt is all wet!" Chrissy shrieked. "And my feet are sticky!"

"Elizabeth," Jessica said, coming into the kitchen, "if you don't cut down on the noise, you'll wake—" She stopped when she saw the orange juice. "Oh, no!" she exclaimed.

Mrs. Wakefield came to the door. "Did I hear Chrissy crying?" she asked. Then she saw Chrissy standing in the middle of a spreading orange puddle. She gave a long sigh. "Hand me the mop, Elizabeth," she said.

Elizabeth shook her head. She had to show her mother that she and Jessica could be responsible, even in the midst of utter disaster! "This isn't your mess, Mom," she replied. "I'll mop."

Jessica held out her hand. "And I'll give Chrissy another bath," she said.

"But I don't want—" Chrissy began.

"You *need* a bath, Chrissy," Mrs. Wakefield said gently. "You're all sticky."

Chrissy didn't argue. She went with Jessica, leaving sticky footprints all the way to the bathroom.

After Jessica bathed her, Chrissy listened while Elizabeth sang two verses of "Puff the Magic Dragon" and read *The Cat That Wouldn't Behave* five times.

"Good night, 'Lizabeth," she said finally as she snuggled down into her blanket. "I love you."

"I love you, too, Chrissy," Elizabeth said. Elizabeth kissed her and then paused. Chrissy looked like an angel with her hair spread out all over the pillow.

"I guess we need another rule," Elizabeth said a few minutes later as she sat down on Jessica's bed. "No phone calls after eight o'clock."

"Not a bad idea," Jessica agreed. "We'll have to tell all our friends." She jumped up. "Hey, would you like to see the new cheers we learned at Boosters practice today?"

Elizabeth sat back on the bed. "Sure," she said, "as long as you don't yell and wake Chrissy up."

"You bet," Jessica agreed. Keeping her voice down almost to a whisper, she went through both cheers.

"Not bad," Elizabeth said approvingly. She stood up and stretched. "It's getting late. I'd better do some homework!"

Suddenly the door to Jessica's room opened and Steven stuck his head in. "You guys better go see what's wrong," he said. "Chrissy's yelling her head off."

Elizabeth and Jessica looked at each other, dismayed. "What could have woken her up this time?" Jessica asked.

"It was probably all that jumping around you were doing up here," Steven replied. "I was in the living room, and it sounded like the ceiling was coming down."

"Oh," Elizabeth said, suddenly understanding. "Jessica, the floor of your room is the ceiling of the den! It was probably your cheering that woke Chrissy up."

Jessica laughed. "I guess we'd better have another rule," she said. Elizabeth giggled and nodded. "No cheering after eight o'clock," they said in unison.

After Jessica had gotten through *The Cat That Wouldn't Behave* four times, Chrissy was finally asleep again. "I didn't even have to *read* the stupid book the last time," Jessica said to Elizabeth as they brushed their teeth. "I know every word by heart."

Elizabeth gave Jessica a half-guilty look. Something had been on her mind all day, and she had to tell Jessica what it was. "Jessica," she said, "I didn't believe you'd ever really take responsibility for Chrissy. But you have. I'm impressed. And I'm sorry for having doubted you."

Jessica smiled. "Thanks. You know, in spite of the way Chrissy behaves sometimes, I still think she's sweet. I love the way she cuddles up while I'm reading to her. But I'm realizing that having her here means giving up a lot of stuff we take for granted."

"It would be that way if we had a new baby in the family, too," Elizabeth added.

Jessica was silent for a moment. Then she said, "Maybe we're not ready for a baby, Elizabeth."

Elizabeth looked seriously at her twin.

"Maybe you're right."

* * *

To Jessica's great surprise, Wednesday morning with Chrissy went smoothly. Chrissy didn't whine while her hair was being braided, and she ate a whole bowl of cornflakes without a fuss. They didn't run into Bruce Patman on the way to the kindergarten, either.

The after-school babysitting went surprisingly well, too. Jessica and Chrissy went to the park to play on the swings, then came home and went to the Howards' to see the fish.

When the girls were leaving the Howards', they ran into Chad. He and Steven had been shooting baskets.

Chad grinned at Jessica. "Hey, Jessica," he said, "don't forget about that dance, huh?"

"I won't," Jessica vowed. How could she forget about Chad Lucas asking her to dance? Excitedly, she ran into the house, got Chrissy some crayons and a coloring book, and headed for the phone in the upstairs hall. Keeping an eye on Chrissy, Jessica called Ellen to tell her what Chad had just said.

"I thought you were going to tell Chad that you're giving him up," Ellen said sternly.

"I know," Jessica replied, "but today wasn't the right time to do it. I couldn't tell him something personal like that in front of Chrissy, could

I?" But the truth was that Jessica was wishing she hadn't decided to reject Chad. He was *so* good-looking. All her friends would die with envy if they saw her dancing with him at Janet's party.

"Well, when, then?" Ellen asked.

"Maybe at the party, after we've danced together," Jessica said. "I don't think Aaron would be *too* mad at me if I only danced with Chad once or twice."

"Jessica Wakefield, that's mean," Ellen replied. "Aaron would be plenty mad. And I wouldn't blame him one bit."

"Well, maybe," Jessica said indecisively, wondering just how mad Aaron was likely to be and whether she really could risk one dance. "But I have to think of Chad. I don't want to break his heart, either."

Ellen paused. "That's true," she said. "Well, let me know what you decide, Jessica."

"I will." Jessica said goodbye just as Elizabeth came up the stairs.

"Looks as if Chrissy is settling down at last," Elizabeth observed, glancing toward the corner where Chrissy was busily coloring.

"She's been great all day," Jessica said affectionately. "Maybe the worst is over." She paused. "Elizabeth, I've got something to ask you."

"What?" Elizabeth asked, sitting down on Jessica's bed.

"It's about Aaron," Jessica said. She climbed onto the bed and crossed her legs. "And Chad."

Elizabeth frowned. "I thought you agreed that Chad was too old for you, Jess."

"I do agree," Jessica admitted. "Basically, I mean. But do you think it would be wrong if I danced with him at Janet's party on Friday night? He asked me."

"Chad Lucas asked you to dance?" Elizabeth eyed her twin incredulously. "I definitely don't think you should dance with him. How would you feel if Aaron danced with some really cute girl?"

"I guess I'd feel jealous," Jessica admitted.

"If Aaron's your boyfriend, you don't need to dance with Chad. And, remember, Chad's way too old!" Elizabeth said firmly.

"But sometimes I wonder if Aaron really *is* my boyfriend," Jessica protested. "I mean, he hasn't kissed me or anything. It's not like you and Todd." Jessica had been very impressed when Elizabeth had told her that Todd had kissed her at the bowling party. For weeks, Jessica had wished that Aaron would kiss her, too, but so far she'd been disappointed.

"I don't know if Todd would agree that just

because a guy kisses a girl, she's his girlfriend," Elizabeth said. Then she lowered her voice. "Chrissy asked him yesterday if he was my boyfriend. He didn't say no, but he didn't say yes, either."

"Well, Todd's wrong!" Jessica exclaimed indignantly. "He kissed you, and that makes you his girlfriend. I don't care *what* he thinks." She leaned forward. "I'll bet Todd's a good kisser," she said softly.

Elizabeth stood up. "Jess, I really don't think you should dance with Chad Lucas, no matter how much he likes you." She glanced at Chrissy, who was still busy coloring. "It's time for me to help Mom with dinner."

"I want to watch Big Bird!" Chrissy piped up.

"Well, come on, then," Jessica said. "You've been such a good girl, you deserve a treat. While you watch Big Bird, I'll make you a snack."

For the rest of the evening, Chrissy behaved perfectly. She played with her dolls while the twins did their homework. Then she took a bath and even let Jessica wash her hair without any trouble.

"It looks like Chrissy's finally come around," Elizabeth said. "She was perfect tonight."

"All it took was a little patience," Jessica said.

Elizabeth laughed. "Jessica Wakefield, that's the first time I've ever heard you talk about being *patient!*"

"I told you, Elizabeth," Jessica said firmly, "I've turned over a new leaf. I'm learning how to be responsible. Now I'm going to finish my homework."

But even though Jessica opened her books, she didn't do much work. She started day-dreaming about dancing with Chad. While they were dancing, Aaron cut in and made her dance with him. He begged her not to have any other boyfriends, and then he kissed her, right in front of Lila and Ellen and everyone else in the room!

On Thursday morning Elizabeth got Chrissy ready for kindergarten. When they came into the kitchen, Jessica and Steven were both there eating their breakfasts. Chrissy climbed up into her chair. "I'll have cornflakes," she announced brightly.

Elizabeth got two bowls from the cupboard.

Chrissy gave Steven a sweet smile. "Hi, Steven," she said. " 'Lizabeth's got a boyfriend."

Elizabeth almost dropped the box of cornflakes.

Steven's eyebrows shot up. "She does?" he asked with a wicked grin. "What's his name?"

Elizabeth felt the red climbing to her cheeks.

Once Steven found out something personal like this, he would tease her unmercifully. Quickly, she said, "Chrissy, would you like a glass of orange juice?"

"His name is Todd," Chrissy continued. "He rides a bike and he's a good kisser."

"He *is*?" Steven chortled. He swung around in his chair. "How about that, Elizabeth? So Todd Wilkins is a good kisser, is he?"

Elizabeth felt like crawling under the table. Chrissy must have listened to and understood her conversation with Jessica the afternoon before! She put a bowl of cereal in front of Chrissy and got her a spoon. "Here's your breakfast," she said.

On the other side of the table, Jessica's face was as white as Elizabeth's was red. Elizabeth knew what her twin was thinking. Chrissy had spilled the beans about Todd. How long would it be before she blabbed to Steven about *Chad?*

But Steven wasn't paying any attention to Jessica. "Tell me, Elizabeth, just how long has this little romance been going on?"

"It's not a little romance," Elizabeth answered, forgetting her resolve to ignore Steven.

"Aha!" Steven shouted. "So it's a *big* romance! Tsk-tsk, Elizabeth."

"That's not what I said!" Elizabeth answered

desperately. Then she sat and fumed silently while Steven continued his relentless, unmerciful teasing.

Finally Steven pushed back his chair and stood up. "I don't know when I've enjoyed breakfast more," he said, laughing. "Thanks, Elizabeth." He leaned over and patted Chrissy on the head. "And thank *you*, kid." On his way out of the kitchen, he turned. "If you've got any other interesting pieces of news, Chrissy," he added, "you can tell me at dinner. I'll be all ears."

"I will," Chrissy promised. "Bye, Steven." She turned to Elizabeth, smiling. "I'm ready to go to kindergarten now, 'Lizabeth."

"Then get your sweater," Elizabeth ordered. She was angry with Steven, but she was just as angry at herself. After what had happened at the park the other day with Todd, she should have known better than to talk about boys in front of Chrissy. She had to face the truth. She simply wasn't ready for a little sister. She wasn't *smart* enough.

Jessica was still sitting on the other side of the table. "Elizabeth," she whispered when Chrissy had gone to get her sweater, "do you think she'll tell Steven about Chad?" She bit her lip anxiously. "If she does, I'll *die* of embarrassment!"

"Who knows what she'll say next?" Elizabeth

said. Suddenly she was angry at Jessica, too, for getting her into this whole mess. "Listen, Jessica," she said hotly, "the next time you get a bright idea about babysitting a five-year-old, let me know in advance. I'll arrange to stay with Amy. And if you've got any more schemes up your sleeve to convince Mom and Dad to have a baby, you can count me out. One sister at a time is all I can handle. Not to mention one brother!"

Jessica looked at her angrily. "You don't need to get mad at *me,* Elizabeth. I'd like to get out of this just as much as you would." She sniffed. "Anyway, I didn't exactly have to twist your arm. You were happy to have Chrissy stay with us."

Elizabeth glared at her twin. Things were going from bad to worse. Chrissy's behavior was threatening to come between the two of them!

Seven

On Thursday afternoon, Amy headed over to work for Mrs. Richards, the daughter of the man she'd worked for on Tuesday. Amy's shoulders were slumped and her feet were dragging. She really didn't want to clean another garage. But she still couldn't think of any other way to make some fast money. When Mrs. Richards came to the door, Amy spoke cheerfully. "Hi, I'm Amy Sutton. I'm here to clean your garage."

"Wonderful!" Mrs. Richards said enthusiastically. "I'm *so* glad you could come, Amy."

Amy was puzzled by Mrs. Richards's enthusiasm. Why so much excitement over a little thing like a garage? But when Amy saw the garage, she understood. It was even worse than Mr. Andretti's had been. It was crammed with boxes, rusty tools, paint cans, broken toys, and assorted junk.

"I was so thrilled when my father told me what a splendid job you did for him," Mrs. Richards gushed. "And for only six dollars!" She frowned at the dirty garage. "I'm afraid ours is a bit messier than his."

Amy hesitated and wondered if she should ask for more money. This garage *was* a lot worse than the other one. But she'd already said she charged six dollars, so without any further discussion she started to haul boxes out of the garage. Following Mrs. Richards's instructions, she set aside several boxes of toys, books, and baby pictures. Before long the garbage cans were so full that Amy had to stack bags around them. Then she swept, organized the shelves, and found a place for everything.

At last Amy was done. Rubbing her sore arms, she went to the back door and knocked. "I'm finished," she announced wearily when Mrs. Richards came to the door.

Together they went out to the garage. "This is marvelous!" Mrs. Richards gushed as she surveyed the garage. "This is stunning! This is—" She stopped. "Where are the baby pictures?"

"Baby pictures?" Amy asked blankly.

"Of course. There was a whole box of them.

They were with the other things I asked you to save."

Amy looked around. "They're probably on one of these shelves," she said. But after a few minutes of searching, it was obvious the baby pictures were nowhere in the garage. "I must have dumped them in the trash by mistake," Amy said miserably.

"That's no problem," Mrs. Richards said pleasantly. "All you have to do is dig them out." Amy bit her lip. Each garbage can was overflowing, and there were at least five bags stacked up beside them.

Amy finally found the box of baby pictures at the very bottom of the very last can. She knocked at Mrs. Richards's door again. "Here's the box," she said wearily.

"And here's your six dollars," Mrs. Richards replied, handing her the bills. "Plus a dollar tip."

Amy pocketed the money and did some quick calculations in her head. She only had about seven dollars left to earn. Two more jobs, and she'd have the money for the soccer tickets plus some left over. But she just wasn't sure she could face two more dirty garages!

By Thursday evening, Jessica was so nervous she thought she'd jump out of her skin. Chrissy had already blabbed to Steven about Elizabeth and Todd. If she told him about Chad, it would be utterly humiliating! And something even worse occurred to her. What if Chrissy said something about Chad in front of her parents? After the Josh Angler episode, Jessica knew she'd never get her parents to believe she hadn't flirted with Chad. She'd probably be grounded for life! Somehow, Chrissy had to be stopped.

Before dinner, Jessica cornered Elizabeth in the hallway outside the kitchen. "Elizabeth," she whispered desperately, "we've got to keep Chrissy from saying anything at dinner about you-know-who. *Both* you-know-whos!"

"I agree," Elizabeth whispered back, glancing toward the kitchen table where Chrissy sat absorbed in a project. "But I don't see how we're going to do that. She's not a puppy. We can't put a muzzle on her."

"But we can monopolize the dinner conversation so she can't get a word in," Jessica replied. "And we can keep her so busy eating that she can't talk."

"Isn't it going to be pretty obvious that we're trying to shut her up?" Elizabeth asked doubtfully.

"Not if we do it right," Jessica said. "Just follow my lead."

Jessica managed to chatter nonstop about

school, the Unicorns, and the Boosters that night at dinner. She never gave Chrissy a chance to get a word in.

Finally, Mrs. Wakefield said, "Jessica, your spaghetti is getting cold." She smiled at Chrissy. "Tell us what you did today, Chrissy."

Quick as a flash, Jessica stuffed a piece of Italian bread into Chrissy's hand. Chrissy took a bite.

When Chrissy opened her mouth to talk, Jessica said firmly, "Chrissy, don't talk with your mouth full."

Mrs. Wakefield nodded. "You can tell us your news when you've finished your bread, Chrissy. How about you, Elizabeth? What was your day like?"

Jessica relaxed a little and managed to take a few bites while Elizabeth talked about her social-studies assignment, the next issue of the *Sixers*, and the book she'd just read.

"Somebody's really wound you girls up this evening," Mr. Wakefield said with a grin when Elizabeth paused for breath. "Your report is fascinating, Elizabeth. But we ought to let Chrissy and Steven tell us what they've been up to today. Chrissy, do you have any news?"

Steven threw Elizabeth a wicked grin. "Chrissy had some interesting news at breakfast," he said. He leaned his elbows on the table. "Do you have anything more to say on that subject?" he encouraged.

"Yes," Chrissy piped up. She beamed at Steven. "Jessica has—"

At that moment Jessica reached for another piece of bread. Her elbow hit Chrissy's milk and knocked it over.

"I'm sorry," Jessica said, but inside she felt very pleased with herself.

Steven gave a disgusted laugh. "I'll bet you are," he said. "Chrissy, what were you about to tell us?"

"It's dripping in my lap!" Chrissy wailed. "My jeans are wet!"

Elizabeth jumped up and pulled back Chrissy's chair. "Come on, Chrissy," she said, "let's get some dry jeans."

"Jessica," Mrs. Wakefield said, "mop up that spilled milk. And please, be more careful."

"I will," Jessica promised meekly. She mopped up the milk while Elizabeth took Chrissy away from the table. Elizabeth returned with Chrissy just in time to sit down for dessert. Fortunately, Steven had already left to meet some of his friends. He was supposed to have taken care of the kitchen chores, but neither of the twins complained about doing his work.

"That was a *close* call," Jessica whispered to Elizabeth as they cleared the table.

"If you hadn't knocked over that milk," Elizabeth whispered back, "who knows what Chrissy might have said?"

"She might have said it anyway," Jessica replied, "if you hadn't gotten her away from the table."

Elizabeth gave a weary sigh. "How many more nights of this do we have to go through?"

"There's only tomorrow evening, and that's the party," Jessica replied. "Mom and Dad are going to watch her, but I don't think she'll say anything without Steven around to egg her on. The Steeles will be picking her up on Saturday, and then we'll be safe." Jessica glanced anxiously at Elizabeth. "Do you think we can keep her quiet and away from Steven until she leaves?"

"We *have* to," Elizabeth replied grimly.

Luckily, Steven didn't come home before Chrissy went to bed. The twins pulled out Steven's old blocks and helped Chrissy build a house. Then they read some of their favorite stories from their old books. When it was time for bed, Chrissy put her arms around Jessica's neck and gave her a kiss. "You're nice, Jessica," she said. "I love you."

Jessica smiled down at the little girl snuggled

under the blanket. She felt considerably more affectionate than she had before dinner. Maybe she had overreacted to the whole thing. Maybe Chrissy hadn't meant to say anything about Chad at all. She smoothed Chrissy's hair.

"You're nice, too," Jessica said. "How'd you like to watch Elizabeth and me get ready for the party tomorrow night?"

Chrissy nodded happily, and drifted off to sleep halfway through "Puff the Magic Dragon."

At school Friday morning, everybody was talking about the party. "What are you wearing, Amy?" Elizabeth asked.

"I haven't had the energy to think about clothes," Amy said tiredly. "I've been thinking about garages."

Elizabeth looked at Amy sympathetically. "How's your business going?" she asked. She giggled when Amy told her about Mrs. Richards and the baby pictures.

Even Amy had to laugh, though her shoulders were still sore from carrying boxes. "Only two more garages and I can buy the tickets," she said with a sigh. "*If* I survive, that is."

On Friday afternoon, while all the other girls hurried home to get ready for the party, Amy went from door to door again, asking people if they wanted their garages cleaned. But she struck out at every house.

By four-thirty, Amy knew she was licked. Even if she got a job right then, she wouldn't have been able to finish it. She'd have to clean *two* garages the next day to make the money she still needed. But what if she couldn't find two garages to clean? Where else could she come up with the money?

Gloomily, Amy trudged home. She didn't have much time to get ready for Janet's party, and she wasn't at all sure what she was going to wear. She couldn't even imagine having fun at the party when she was so preoccupied. If only someone would suddenly offer to *give* her some money!

It was four-thirty on Friday afternoon and Mr. and Mrs. Wakefield hadn't gotten home from work yet. But the twins weren't worried. They were too excited about the party. Jessica was on the phone with Ellen, discussing her outfit. Ellen reminded her that that night was the night she had said she would tell Chad she was giving him up for another boy, but Jessica brushed off the reminder. She didn't want to think about that just yet.

Humming to herself, Jessica opened her makeup kit and began to sort through it. She'd be wearing her favorite turquoise dress, so she decided to wear a tiny smudge of turquoise eye shadow, pale pink lip gloss, a teeny bit of blush, rose-scented perfume, and, of course, some rose-pink nail polish. Finally she pulled out a bottle of hand lotion, and carefully arranged all the little bottles and pots in front of her.

The phone rang again and Jessica dashed out into the hall to answer it. This time it was Lila, wanting to know whether she should wear white sandals or white patent-leather pumps.

"White pumps are much more elegant," Jessica said. "And I think Jake would like you better in white pumps."

Just then Steven tapped Jessica on the shoulder. "What do you want? I'm talking to Lila," Jessica said irritably.

"I'm sure you and Lila are talking about something absolutely crucial," Steven said with a grin. "But I think you'd better see what Chrissy's gotten herself into."

"I have to go, Lila," Jessica said hurriedly. She put the receiver back in its cradle and dashed into her room. Then she stopped short. "Chrissy, what have you done?" she cried.

"I'm getting pretty," Chrissy said happily, waving a little sponge. "Like you."

For a moment Jessica thought she was going

to be sick. Chrissy's mouth was smeared with lip gloss and she had blush from her forehead to her chin. Both eyes were smudged with turquoise eye shadow, and her hands were sticky with hand lotion. Worse, Jessica's bedspread was stained with a big smear of nail polish, and her turquoise dress was dotted with blotches of makeup.

"I can't *believe* this!" Jessica cried hopelessly. Not only had Chrissy ruined her bedspread and her dress, but her makeup as well.

"Neither could I, when I saw what she'd done," Steven said. "You should have kept an eye on her, Jessica."

"But I was just out in the hall," Jessica wailed, "and only for a minute." Suddenly she turned on Chrissy and exploded. "Chrissy, you are a *bad* girl!" She stamped her foot. "Bad, bad, *bad!*"

Chrissy's face puckered up. "I'm not bad!" she cried, flinging herself onto Steven. "I'm good! Steven says so. I'll be *his* little sister instead!"

Steven laughed. "Sure, I like you, kid. You're not bad—at least, not *all* bad. In fact, you're pretty useful to have around." He arched his eyebrows at Jessica. "You don't *really* think somebody like Chad Lucas could have a crush on you, do you?"

Jessica felt like her heart had just dropped to her stomach. Chrissy had told Steven about Chad!

"Of course, a story like this is just a *tiny* bit hard for me to swallow," Steven went on. "I'll have to check it out at the source."

"The source?" Jessica asked, horrified.

"Chad, of course," Steven said casually.

"Steven, *please* don't talk to Chad about this!" Jessica hated to plead with her brother, but it was the only thing she could do.

"Why not?" Steven asked. He looked at her skeptically. "Did you make it up? Are you afraid he'll laugh at the idea of having a crush on my baby sister?"

"Of course I didn't make it up," Jessica said, stung. "It's true. It's just that . . . I'm afraid he'll be embarrassed," she finished.

Steven guffawed. "You're worried about *Chad* being embarrassed?" He laughed again. "Chrissy says you're also worried about Aaron being mad at you."

Jessica moaned. Chrissy had packed a lot of information into the little chat she'd had with Steven.

"I wonder what Aaron will say when he finds out?"

"Aaron?" Jessica gulped.

"Sure," Steven said. "Doesn't he have a right to know what's been going on behind his back?"

"Steven!" Jessica cried. "You *wouldn't!*"

"Just wait and see," Steven teased. "Thanks again, kid," he said to Chrissy, and patted her on the head before he went out the door.

Chrissy smiled at Jessica. "See?" she said triumphantly. "Steven likes me."

"Well, if he does," Jessica fumed, "he's the *only* one!"

Eight

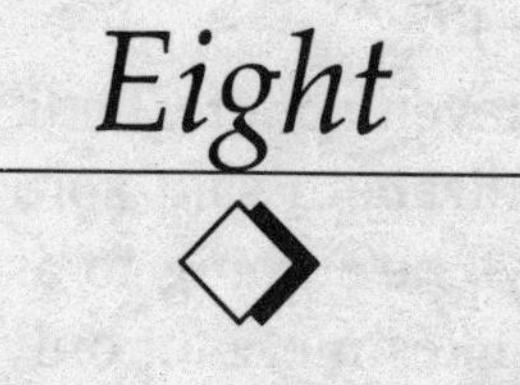

Elizabeth had bought a new bar of lilac-scented soap, and she was enjoying her shower. When she was finished, she wrapped herself in a soft towel and dusted her shoulders with lilac powder, thinking about the party all the while. She hadn't talked to Todd since the episode with Chrissy in the park, and she was hoping that they could clear things up tonight.

Still wrapped in the towel, Elizabeth opened the door to Jessica's room. What she saw made her gasp. Jessica stood in the middle of the floor, crying furiously. Chrissy sat on the bed, and she was crying, too. The tears made a streaky mess on her brightly colored face.

"Jessica!" Elizabeth exclaimed. "Why are you crying? And what's Chrissy got all over her face?"

Jessica pointed at Chrissy. "I'm crying because of that spoiled brat!" she shrieked. "She's ruined my life!"

Elizabeth surveyed the scene. "Chrissy's trashed your stuff all right, but I don't see how it's ruined your life."

"She told Steven about Chad!" Jessica moaned.

"Uh-oh," Elizabeth said softly.

"Steven says he's going to ask Chad whether it's true that he likes me. Not only that, he's going to tell Aaron about Chad!" Jessica began sobbing again.

"I'm sure Steven was teasing about telling Aaron. He isn't mean enough to do a thing like that."

"He said he was going to," Jessica insisted. She yanked a tissue from a box and blew her nose. "I'm not going to the party."

"You *have* to go!" Elizabeth said firmly. "You can't let Steven bully you into hiding out at home!"

"I *can't* go!" Jessica cried. "It would be too awful!" She pointed at Chrissy. "Anyway, that little monster has ruined my dress."

"I'm not a little monster," Chrissy shouted. "I'm *good!* Steven says so!"

"Forget about what Steven says," Jessica replied. "He's a liar."

Elizabeth picked up Jessica's dress. "There's really only a little blush here, Jessica," she said. "I'm sure you can brush it out."

"It doesn't matter," Jessica interrupted. "I won't be wearing it. I'm not going to the party."

"Yes, you are," Elizabeth commanded. "It may be uncomfortable and embarrassing, but you *have* to go. If you don't, everybody will know why. If Steven talks to Aaron, you have to be there to explain."

It took all of Elizabeth's coaxing and convincing skills, but eventually Jessica agreed. "This party's going to be the worst experience of my life," she sighed, "but I guess you're right. Staying away would make things worse." She glared at Chrissy. "It's all your fault! I wish you'd get lost!"

Elizabeth frowned. "We can't blame Chrissy for everything, Jessica. After all, she's only five. We should have known better than to talk about private stuff in front of her."

Jessica blew her nose again. "Well, I can't imagine anything worse than having a big brother like Steven," she muttered. "Unless it's having a little sister like Chrissy. Between the two of them, they've made my life miserable!"

Elizabeth was cleaning Chrissy's face and hands and Jessica was cleaning the blush off her dress when the phone rang.

"It's probably Lila," Jessica said glumly. "She wasn't sure her father could drive her to Janet's, and she said she'd call if she needed a ride. You answer it, Elizabeth. I don't want to talk to her right now. Tell her I'm sick," Jessica said theatrically, "or tell her I'm dead, or in the shower. Tell her anything—but *don't* tell her the truth!"

Elizabeth suppressed a smile at Jessica's dramatics. She hurried to the phone. It was Mrs. Wakefield.

"Hi, Mom," Elizabeth said. "We're getting ready to go to the party. What time will you be home?"

"That's what I'm calling about, Elizabeth," Mrs. Wakefield said soberly. "Something important has come up on this new job, and I have to work late. I've already talked to your father. He's agreed to take you to the party and stay with Chrissy. He's just leaving the office now."

"OK," Elizabeth replied. " I'm sorry you have to work late, Mom."

Elizabeth returned to Jessica's bedroom. "It was Mom," she reported to Jessica. "She's working late tonight, so Dad will take us to the party and babysit with Chrissy."

"Elizabeth, are you *sure* it's a good idea for me to go to the party?" Jessica asked, sighing.

"Maybe you should just say I'm sick. I don't see how I can face anyone!"

"You *have* to," Elizabeth replied firmly. "Anyway, it might not be as bad as you think. Maybe Steven was just giving you a hard time. Stop worrying and get dressed. Dad will be here in a little while."

A half-hour later, Elizabeth glanced at her watch. "I wonder what's keeping Dad," she said. "It doesn't take thirty minutes to drive from his office to our house."

"Maybe he stopped at the store," Jessica suggested.

The phone rang in the hall, and Jessica picked it up. "It's Dad," she told her twin. "Where are you?" she asked. "Elizabeth and I are ready." She listened for a moment, then yelled, "But that could take *hours!*"

Elizabeth came up behind her. "What's the matter?" she asked anxiously.

"The van's broken down, and Dad has to wait for the tow truck," Jessica told her, turning away from the phone.

"That's no problem," Elizabeth said. "We can ride to the party with Amy."

Jessica brightened and turned back to the phone. "Don't worry about us, Dad. And I hope you don't have to wait too long for the tow truck." She said goodbye and hung up.

Suddenly Elizabeth gasped. "Chrissy!" she cried. "We forgot about Chrissy! If Dad's stuck, there's nobody to take care of her!"

"Let's call Mom," Jessica said. "She can go get Dad."

Elizabeth shook her head. "That new job she's working on is really important. She can't leave the office now."

"That settles it," Jessica said dismally to Elizabeth. "You go to the party. I'll stay home with Chrissy."

Elizabeth shook her head. She had been looking forward to the party because it meant she'd be able to talk to Todd. But she didn't *have* to go, and Jessica did. "It's more important for you to go to the party. I'll stay home with Chrissy."

"But Elizabeth," Jessica cried, "I can't face Chad and Aaron without your moral support!"

"You'll have to," Elizabeth said sadly. "There's no other way. Somebody's got to babysit Chrissy."

Chrissy had wandered out into the hall where the twins were talking. "Are you babysitting me?" she asked, looking up at Elizabeth.

"I guess," Elizabeth said, frowning. "Unless—"

"Unless what?" Jessica asked.

Elizabeth's face brightened. "Unless we can hire a babysitter."

"Hire one?" Jessica asked. "But who?"

"I know who!" Elizabeth said. "Amy!" She picked up the phone. "Why didn't I think of this before?"

"But she's going to the party," Jessica objected.

Elizabeth waited for Amy to answer the phone. "I know. But she needs money for those soccer tickets. I'll bet she'll be glad to do it. Cross your fingers and hope she hasn't already left."

Amy was getting dressed. Even after her shower, she still wasn't in a party mood. Her hair didn't look right, and she didn't like the outfit she'd picked. "For two cents," she grumbled at her reflection in the mirror, "I'd stay home."

Out in the hall the phone rang. It was Elizabeth.

"What's up?" Amy asked.

"Mom and Dad were supposed to babysit Chrissy tonight," Elizabeth said. "But Mom has to work, and our van broke down and Dad can't get home."

"Do you and Jessica need a ride?" Amy asked.

"No," Elizabeth said. "What we need is a babysitter."

"Hey," Amy exclaimed happily, "how about me?"

"Are you sure, Amy?" Elizabeth asked. "It would mean that you'd have to miss the party, but Jessica and I would be glad to pay you."

Amy didn't hesitate. "How much?"

"How much do you want?" Elizabeth asked.

"Seven dollars," Amy replied. "I know it's a lot," she added, "but that's about what I need to buy the soccer tickets. I can't do it for any less."

There was muffled whispering on the other end of the line, and then Elizabeth said, "We'll pay it. Come over as soon as you can."

"I'm on my way." As she hurried out the door, she was thinking happily to herself, *No more garages!*

"I'll pay half and you can pay half," Elizabeth said to Jessica after she'd put down the phone. "You *do* have three-fifty, don't you?"

Jessica nodded. "But I'm still not sure this is the best thing, Elizabeth. Maybe I should just stay home and—"

"Not *you*, Jessica," Chrissy said loudly. "I don't want you. You're mean. You yell at me."

She put her hand into Elizabeth's and gave her an angelic smile. "I want 'Lizabeth to babysit me."

Elizabeth knelt down. "My friend Amy will stay with you. You'll be a good girl, won't you?"

Chrissy's face puckered up. "No, I won't!" she cried. "I don't want a babysitter! I want you!"

"But she'll play games with you, and fix a snack, and let you watch TV," Elizabeth said. "And tomorrow morning, Jessica and I will tell you all about the party. OK?"

"No!" Chrissy screamed. She was still saying no when Amy arrived.

"I'm afraid this isn't going to be easy," Elizabeth told Amy.

"It's got to be easier than cleaning out garages," Amy said. She walked toward Chrissy and held out her hand. "Hi, Chrissy. I'm Amy. Let's go to the kitchen and get a snack."

"No!" Chrissy yelled again. "No, no, *no!*"

Elizabeth sighed. "I really feel guilty sticking you with a rotten job like this," she said. "Sometimes Chrissy's a lot of fun, but right now she's being a pain."

"Hey, don't feel guilty," Amy said. "You guys are paying plenty for my time. Anyway, if I don't babysit tonight, I'll have to clean out garages tomorrow. Call it even." She shrugged. "I wasn't too thrilled about the party to begin with. When you phoned, I was just thinking that I might stay home anyway."

"Well," Elizabeth said, "I guess Jessica and I should be going."

"OK," Amy said, then went on brightly, "Chrissy and I are going to have lots of fun. Aren't we, Chrissy?"

"No!" Chrissy shrieked.

"Does she know any other words?" Amy asked.

Jessica grunted. "She knows too many words."

"What's that supposed to mean?" Amy asked.

"It means," Elizabeth said unhappily, "that Chrissy told Steven some personal stuff about us. About Todd and me, and about Jessica and Chad and Aaron."

Amy's eyes widened. "Wow," she breathed. "That bad?"

"That bad," Jessica confirmed. She glared at Chrissy, who was still yelling. "Chrissy, if you don't shut up, I'm going to tell Amy not to sing 'Puff the Magic Dragon.' "

Chrissy didn't stop yelling, but she lowered the volume a little.

Amy raised her eyebrows. "You mean I have to perform? Maybe I should ask for more money."

Elizabeth sighed. "I guess we could pay you more," she said, "if you really—"

Amy held up her hand and laughed. "I was just kidding," she said. " 'Puff the Magic Dragon' isn't so bad."

"It isn't the singing," Jessica said, "it's the reading that gets you. Have you ever heard of *The Cat That Wouldn't Behave*?"

Amy shook her head. "I don't mind reading, either," she said. "Have fun, and don't worry about a thing. Chrissy and I will be just fine. Won't we, Chrissy?"

"*No!*" Chrissy roared.

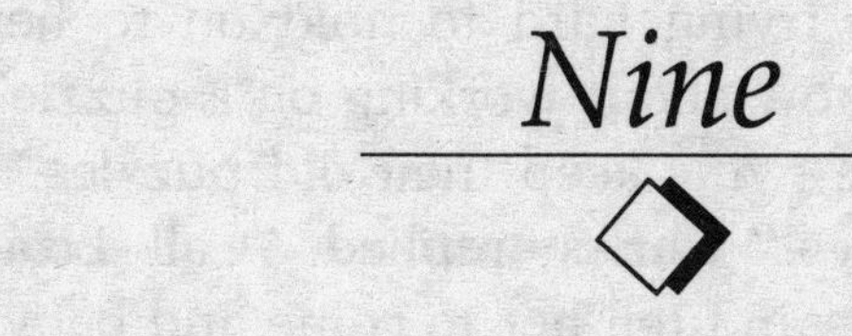

Nine

After the twins had left, Amy realized that she was going to earn every penny of her seven dollars. It took almost twenty minutes and every babysitting trick she knew to coax Chrissy out of her sulk and into the kitchen for a peanut-butter sandwich, a glass of milk, and some cookies. Chrissy's snack took up about twenty minutes.

"Well, Chrissy," Amy asked brightly, "what do you think we should do next?"

"I want 'Lizabeth to come home," Chrissy said.

"If you brought your dolls," Amy suggested, "we could play with them."

"You can't play with my dolls!" Chrissy said firmly. "They're *mine!*"

"OK," Amy replied. "*You* can play with

them, then, and I'll watch." She held out her hand. "Come on, Chrissy, show me your dolls."

Chrissy put her hands behind her back and stuck out her chin stubbornly. "I'll only play dolls with 'Lizabeth."

Amy sighed, trying hard to hold on to her patience. "Well, how about working on a puzzle? I know where the twins keep their old puzzles."

"I hate puzzles," Chrissy replied. "Call 'Lizabeth on the phone and tell her to come and babysit me!"

Amy shook her head. "I can't do that, Chrissy," she explained. "Elizabeth and Jessica are paying me to stay with you." No matter how hard it was to handle Chrissy, it was still terrific luck that the twins needed a babysitter at the very moment that she needed money. "I need money so I can buy a present for my parents," she added.

Chrissy gave Amy a cagey look. "I've got a quarter," she said. "I'll give it to you if you call 'Lizabeth."

Amy couldn't help but laugh. "You're pretty clever for a five-year-old," she said. "But I'm *not* calling Elizabeth, and that's that." She looked at her watch. "It's seven-thirty, time for my favorite TV show. Want to watch it with me?"

"No," Chrissy said. And to every other suggestion Amy made, she also answered no, no, no.

Finally, just as Amy was beginning to feel really desperate, she hit on Chrissy's favorite game, hide-and-seek.

"Well, maybe," Chrissy said slowly when Amy suggested it. "But I'll only play if you let me hide."

Amy sighed gratefully. At last she'd discovered something that Chrissy liked to do! "Sure, you can hide," she agreed. She covered her eyes and started to count to a hundred.

For the next half-hour, Amy and Chrissy played hide-and-seek. But Chrissy couldn't seem to find any good hiding places.

"You're too easy to find, Chrissy," Amy said after she had found Chrissy in Mrs. Wakefield's closet, under Elizabeth's bed, and behind the TV set in the den. "You have to think of better places to hide."

"Can I hide *anywhere?*" Chrissy asked eagerly.

"Anywhere," Amy told her. "Hide where I'd *never* think of looking for you."

"I will," Chrissy said, with the first smile Amy had seen. "I'll hide where you'll never find me." And she ran off as Amy started to count.

Everybody at Janet's party seemed to be having fun. Everybody, that is, but Jessica. Twenty minutes after they arrived, Elizabeth found Jessica standing beside the refreshment table in the living room, looking uncomfortable. "Have you talked to Chad yet?" Elizabeth whispered.

"No," Jessica said. "He didn't get here until just a few minutes ago." She gave a little nod. "He's over there by the window, talking to Cathy Connors."

"Steven hasn't talked to him, either?" Elizabeth asked hopefully.

"I don't think so," Jessica replied. Then her eyes widened. "But there's Steven now!" she whispered, grabbing Elizabeth's arm. "He's heading straight for Chad!"

Chad and Steven started talking.

"I've *got* to know what Steven's telling him!" Jessica said urgently. "If I knew, I could figure out what to do. Elizabeth, go out on the patio and crouch below the window. It'll be easy to hear them from there."

Elizabeth frowned. She didn't like the idea of listening in on somebody's private conversation. "If it's so easy, why don't *you* do it?"

"Because Steven's looking at me," Jessica replied. "He knows I'm dying to hear what he's saying. But he'd never believe that *you'd* eavesdrop."

"I can't believe it, either," Elizabeth said.

"Hurry," Jessica urged. "Or it'll be all over

before you get there! Anyway, Steven doesn't have any right to talk to Chad about me. It's not any of his business."

Elizabeth had to agree that Jessica was right. Steven shouldn't be telling Chad something he found out from Chrissy. Carrying her soda, she wandered out to the patio, trying to look as if she didn't have anything special in mind. There was a bench just beneath the open living-room window, and she hunched down on it. She could make out Steven's voice.

"You know little sisters," he said with a laugh. "They get screwy ideas sometimes."

Chad didn't laugh. "I'm really sorry," he said. Elizabeth thought he sounded embarrassed. "I never dreamed your sister would think I wanted her for a girlfriend. She's cute, and I thought it was neat having her around." He paused. "You know, sort of like having a little sister."

A little sister! That wasn't at all the way Jessica had imagined it! She would be terribly hurt and embarrassed when she discovered the truth. Elizabeth started to sneak away. She'd better find Jessica and tell her right away, before—

But then Steven started to speak again, and she sat back down. His voice had lost its patronizing tone. "When Chrissy told me that Jessica thought you had a crush on her, Chad, I really gave her a hard time. In fact, I probably overdid the teasing."

"That's too bad," Chad said regretfully. "I'd hate to think Jessica got hurt because I gave her the wrong idea."

"That's why I was hoping," Steven said hesitantly, "that you'd dance with her and let her know that she's an OK kid. You know, kind of let her down easy."

Suddenly Elizabeth felt sorry for her thoughts about Steven. He wasn't a bad brother after all. He really *did* care about his sisters.

Chad was silent for a moment, and Elizabeth waited anxiously for his response. "Yeah, I guess you're right," he said finally. "I guess I owe it to Jessica to do the decent thing. Anyway, I *did* ask her for a dance. Have you seen her around?"

"She's over by the refreshment table," Steven said.

Elizabeth stood up. Maybe if she hurried, she could get to Jessica first and clue her in. But as she turned to go back inside she bumped into Todd.

"Hi, Elizabeth," Todd said. "Listen, I—"

"Could we talk later, Todd?" Elizabeth asked hurriedly. "I have to see Jessica about something really important."

"Sure," Todd said with a friendly smile. "Anyway, I'm heading for the rec room with some of the other guys to see Joe's model railroad. See you later, OK?"

"OK," Elizabeth agreed. Then she hurried back into the living room, where she had left Jessica. But she was too late. Just as she stepped inside the door she saw Chad go up to Jessica, smile, and say something. Jessica smiled back. Then he took her hand and walked with her to where some of the kids were dancing.

Ellen Riteman and Lila Fowler were standing nearby, talking in low voices. They didn't notice Elizabeth behind them. "Do you *really* believe that Chad's got a crush on Jessica?" Elizabeth heard Lila ask Ellen skeptically.

"I heard him ask her to dance with him," Ellen said. "And he comes over to her house a lot." She looked around worriedly. "I wonder where Aaron is. I hope he doesn't see them dancing together."

"I think he's in the rec room looking at Joe's railroad," Lila said. She tilted her head as she watched Chad and Jessica dance. "If I were in her shoes," she sighed, "I'd have a hard time deciding. Chad is cuter than Aaron. And he's more popular."

"But he's a lot older," Ellen reminded Lila. "And you know the trouble Jessica got into the last time she got mixed up with an older guy."

She leaned forward. "They're talking. She must be letting him down at this very moment!"

Elizabeth saw that Jessica and Chad were so deep in conversation they were barely moving. She couldn't see Chad's face, but she thought Jessica looked startled. Then Chad swung her around so that Elizabeth couldn't see Jessica's face. Chad looked very troubled.

"See how serious he looks?" Ellen exclaimed. "She must have told him!"

Then Chad leaned over and kissed Jessica softly on the cheek. The music ended, and he walked away.

"He kissed her!" Lila exclaimed. "In front of everyone!"

Ellen clasped her hands. "How romantic! I can't wait to hear what he said when she told him!"

"Hi, Elizabeth." Sophia Rizzo approached, smiling. "How about a game of Ping-Pong?"

"Come on, Elizabeth," Brooke Dennis coaxed. "We're organizing a tournament, and we need you."

Elizabeth wanted to stay and hear what Jessica would tell Lila and Ellen. But Brooke and Sophia were tugging at her and she couldn't say no. Anyway, she'd get to hear all about it from Jessica later at home.

* * *

Elizabeth had just walked away with her friends when Jessica left the dance floor, trying not to look as horribly humiliated as she felt. The last few minutes had been the most awful of her entire life. Of course, Chad had been very sweet and apologetic about the whole thing. He'd said he was sorry for the way things had been misunderstood, and he'd given her a farewell, big-brother kiss.

Jessica bit her lip. But no matter what Chad had said, she knew that it was all *her* fault, not his. *She* was the one who had tricked herself into believing that he had a crush on her, when he only liked her as a little sister! What would Lila and Ellen say when they found out what an idiot she'd been? Jessica looked around. She had to find Elizabeth and tell her she had an awful headache and wanted to go straight home. That way she wouldn't have to talk to anybody.

But before Jessica could locate Elizabeth, Lila and Ellen came hurrying up to her. "We saw the whole thing, Jessica," Lila said breathlessly.

Jessica's heart did a backflip. "You saw it?" she asked. Had they heard the awful, humiliating truth?

"Yes," Ellen said, gesturing dramatically. "We

saw everything, right down to the kiss. But unfortunately, we couldn't hear a single word. You have to tell us what you said, and what *he* said!"

"Tell us, Jessica!" Lila commanded eagerly. "We want to hear every detail!"

Then Jessica understood. Lila and Ellen had seen Chad kiss her, but they didn't have a clue as to what he'd said to her. She looked at her feet.

"We just said good-bye," she said modestly. That was true. At the end, after he'd kissed her, he'd said, "Good-bye, Jessica."

"But you talked for a *long* time," Ellen protested. "And we could see how serious Chad looked. Was he heartbroken when you told him? What did he say?"

"He said he was sorry for the way things turned out," Jessica said, again truthfully. "He said that from now on, he'd like to think of me as a sister."

"A *sister*," Ellen cried, rolling her eyes. "Jessica, it sounds like a line from a wonderfully sad romantic movie! What else did he say?"

"I really can't tell you," Jessica said. "It's very private."

"But he *kissed* you," Ellen cried. "The kiss says it all, doesn't it, Lila?"

"Yes, it does," Lila said firmly. "You can keep your lips sealed if you like, Jessica. But Ellen and I know the truth. C'mon, Jessica." Lila took Jessica's arm. "You need some food. You've had a hard night."

"Where's Aaron?" Jessica asked after they had eaten.

"And where's Rick?" Ellen asked, looking around. "I haven't seen him yet."

"I think Aaron and Rick are in the rec room with Jake, looking at Joe's model railroad," Lila said. "Let's go find them and get them to dance."

The Howells had an enormous recreation room. On the floor along one wall, Janet's brother had set up an expensive model-railroad layout. A dozen boys were crowded around it.

Jessica found Aaron and came up behind him. "Hi, Aaron," she said.

"Hi, Jessica," Aaron replied absently. He didn't take his eyes off a miniature train zipping around the track.

"Looks like you're having fun," Jessica remarked. She stood a little closer. "Would you like to dance?"

"This is the most terrific railroad I've ever seen!" Aaron said enthusiastically. He pushed a button and the train screeched to a stop so another locomotive could switch from a siding onto the main track. "It's a lot more fun than dancing. I could run this thing all night!"

And that's exactly what he did. While Jessica fretted and fumed, Aaron played with Joe's train. So did all the other middle-school boys, including Rick Hunter and Jake Hamilton.

A half-hour later, Lila called it quits, looking disgusted. "This party's a disaster," she said. "We might as well go home. I didn't get all dressed up to watch a bunch of guys play with a toy train."

"To think I spent hours getting ready," Ellen said sadly, "and Rick hasn't even noticed me. It's humiliating for the boys to pay more attention to the trains than to us. I'll call my mother. Are you ready, Jessica?"

"I'm ready," Jessica agreed. "A party is no fun if the boys won't dance with us. But I have to find Elizabeth first." A few minutes later she located her twin in the Howells' garage, playing Ping-Pong with a group of girls.

"Elizabeth," Jessica said, "I'm ready to go home."

"Already?" Elizabeth asked, looking surprised. "But it's so early! I haven't had a chance to talk to Todd yet."

Jessica gave a disgruntled laugh. "Forget that," she said. "Todd's with the rest of the guys.

They're too busy playing with Joe's trains to pay any attention to us."

At that moment Todd came into the garage. "Hi, Elizabeth," he said. "Is the tournament over yet? How about getting something to eat?"

Elizabeth looked at Jessica. "I'm not quite ready to go yet," she said.

"If you want a ride home, Elizabeth, my mom will be glad to take you," Todd offered.

"Do you mind?" Elizabeth asked Jessica.

Jessica shrugged. "Why should I mind?" she asked, trying hard not to show her envy.

Ten

When Jessica walked into the house, Amy was standing in the downstairs hallway with the telephone in her hand. Her hair was rumpled, as if she'd been tugging at it with her fingers. Her eyes darted frantically to Jessica.

"Jessica!" Amy cried. She put the telephone down. "Am I glad to see *you!* Where's Elizabeth?"

"She's still at the party," Jessica said. She looked around. "Where's Chrissy?"

"That's why I'm so relieved to see you," Amy said. "I don't *know* where Chrissy is! I've looked for the last half-hour and I can't find her anywhere. I was just calling the police."

The police! This was serious. Jessica frowned. "Where did you lose her?"

"I didn't lose her," Amy said. "She hid. We

were playing hide-and-seek, and I kept finding her. So I told her to hide somewhere I'd never find her. I guess she did, because I searched high and low and I never *did* find her."

"Did you look in the basement?" Jessica asked. "How about my dad's workshop?"

"I looked in the basement, the workshop, the garage—every nook and cranny of the entire house. I yelled 'home free' until I was blue in the face. No Chrissy." Amy bit her lip. "Should we call the police?"

"Not yet," Jessica said calmly. "She's probably in a closet or under a bed. Or maybe she's moving around, hiding somewhere you've already looked."

But a few minutes later Jessica wasn't quite as confident. Either Chrissy had found the best place in the world to hide—or something dreadful had happened to her. Jessica thought guiltily about the angry things she'd said to Chrissy earlier that evening. She'd called Chrissy a monster. And worst of all, she'd said, "I wish you'd get lost." Now she felt ashamed of herself. Chrissy hadn't meant to do any serious harm. She'd just acted the way all little children act.

"It's nine-thirty," Amy said, looking anxiously at her watch. "Do you think we should call the police now?"

Jessica sighed. "Maybe," she said. "I just wish Mom and Dad were here. They'd know what to do."

As if in answer to her wish, Mr. and Mrs. Wakefield arrived at that moment. It only took a minute for Jessica to tell them what had happened.

"Are you *sure* you've looked everywhere?" Mr. Wakefield asked.

"Everywhere!" Jessica and Amy said in unison.

"Everywhere but outside," Jessica added.

"Do you think she might have hidden outdoors, Amy?" Mrs. Wakefield asked.

Amy chewed on her fingernail. "I didn't think so at first," she replied. "It was already dark outside, and most kids are afraid of the dark."

"Chrissy's not afraid of anything," Jessica said proudly, remembering Elizabeth's story of how Chrissy had kicked Bruce Patman.

"But if she'd hidden outside, she would surely have come in by now," Mr. Wakefield said.

"I think we should look around the yard anyway," Mrs. Wakefield said.

With flashlights in hand, they all went outside and searched the yard. But they couldn't find a trace of Chrissy. It was as if she had vanished into thin air.

* * *

Elizabeth and Todd had had a great time talking, dancing, and playing Ping-Pong with everyone. Now they sat out on the patio to talk to each other.

"I'm really glad you didn't go home with Jessica," Todd told Elizabeth. "I've had a good time tonight." He looked at his feet. "Something's been on my mind, Elizabeth. The other day at the park, Chrissy gave me a chance to say how much I like you. I guess I blew it."

Elizabeth could feel her cheeks getting red. "I wish Chrissy hadn't put us on the spot that way," she said.

Todd looked up and reached for her hand. "Yeah, me, too. But I want you to know that I *do* like you, Elizabeth. Better than anybody else. If somebody calls me your boyfriend, I don't mind."

Elizabeth could feel her heart thudding. "Thank you," she said happily, liking the way her hand felt in his. "I like you, too. And I've had a *wonderful* time tonight."

Todd went inside to call his mother to pick them up. Elizabeth thought about the evening while she waited for him. It made her feel warm inside to know that Todd considered himself her boyfriend. It had turned out to be a perfect night.

But when Todd's mother pulled up in front of

the Wakefield house a little while later, Elizabeth quickly realized that everything *wasn't* perfect. Her mother and father were in the yard with flashlights, peering through the bushes.

Hastily, Elizabeth said goodnight to Todd and his mother and ran to her parents. "What's wrong?" she asked. "Have you lost something?"

"Yes," Mr. Wakefield replied. "We've lost Chrissy."

"Chrissy?" Elizabeth exclaimed, dismayed.

Amy came up to Elizabeth and explained the whole story. "I'm really sorry, Elizabeth. I feel as if it's all my fault. If I had been more careful—" She blinked hard, trying to keep back the tears.

"It's not your fault, Amy," Elizabeth comforted her. "Chrissy is hard to manage sometimes. I'm sure you did the best you could." She swallowed the lump that was growing in her throat. "But I should have stayed home and taken care of her. *I'm* the one who is responsible."

"Jessica is responsible, too," Mrs. Wakefield reminded Elizabeth.

Mr. Wakefield frowned. "Speaking of Jessica, where *is* she? I haven't seen her for the last few minutes."

Just then Jessica came out of the dark, holding Chrissy's hand. "Here's Chrissy!"

"Chrissy!" Mrs. Wakefield cried. She gathered the little girl into her arms. "Where have you been?"

"I was hiding," Chrissy said, blinking sleepily. She rubbed her eyes. "Then I got tired of waiting for Amy to find me and I fell asleep." She looked up at Jessica. "Thanks for finding me, Jessica."

"Where *did* you find her, Jessica?" Amy asked.

Jessica looked pleased with herself. "She was at the Howards'," she said, "curled up in front of the aquarium."

"But the Howards aren't home," Elizabeth said. "They went out at the same time we went to the party. I saw them drive off."

"They left their back door unlocked," Jessica explained, "and Chrissy opened it and went in. She was on the floor, sound asleep."

"I wanted to see the zebrafish," Chrissy explained. "Mrs. Howard said I could come anytime. And Amy told me I could hide anywhere I wanted."

Amy laughed. "Didn't I tell you, Elizabeth? Some kids are smarter than we give them credit for."

"Jessica," Mrs. Wakefield said, "I'm really glad you thought about looking at the Howards'.

If you hadn't, it might have been hours before Chrissy was found."

Chrissy held out her arms to Jessica. "I don't think you're mean anymore, Jessica."

Jessica picked Chrissy up and held her tight. "And I don't think you're a little monster," she said, burying her face in Chrissy's hair. "I'm sorry I told you to get lost."

"I don't think you're a little monster, either," Amy told Chrissy with a laugh. "But I have to admit that babysitting you is a lot harder than cleaning people's dirty garages. I've earned every nickle of my money."

Elizabeth smiled. "Speaking of money, Amy, I guess we owe you."

"Seven dollars," Amy said happily. "But next time I decide to buy a present for my parents, I think I'll stick with something that doesn't cost as much as soccer tickets. Collecting cans, baking cookies, mowing lawns, cleaning garages, babysitting—if you ask me, that's a *lot* of work. I'm glad this week is over and my life can get back to normal."

"Me, too," Elizabeth agreed. Chrissy was a sweet little girl, but she was relieved her visit was almost over. When Chrissy was gone, they could go back to watching television after eight o'clock, getting evening phone calls, and doing cheers in their bedrooms if they wanted to. Having a little sister was fun, but only if she was a *temporary* little sister!

That night Chrissy was so sleepy that one verse of "Puff the Magic Dragon" did the trick. Elizabeth and Jessica went into the kitchen for some hot chocolate Mrs. Wakefield had left them. Elizabeth opened the refrigerator and took out ingredients for sandwiches.

"What I want to know," she said, "is what Chad said to you out there on the dance floor."

"And what *I* want to know," Jessica said, putting a plate of cookies on the table, "is what you heard when you listened in on Steven's conversation with Chad."

Elizabeth told her side of the story first, including how she had changed her mind about Steven. "He was really worried about you, Jessica," she said. "He didn't want you to get hurt."

Jessica looked surprised. "Maybe I'll have to change my opinion of older brothers," she said. Then she told her side of the story. Normally, Elizabeth didn't approve of Jessica deliberately fooling her friends. But this time, Jessica had really done nothing wrong. She had saved her pride simply by letting Lila and Ellen think what they wanted to think.

When the girls had finished sharing their stories, Elizabeth leaned forward. "I have to apologize to you again, Jessica," she said.

"Apologize?" Jessica asked, helping herself to a cookie. "What for?"

"For thinking that you wouldn't do your part to take care of Chrissy. When we made up that list at the beginning of the week, I figured that I'd end up doing all your work. But now the week is over and you did every bit of your share."

"I agree," Mrs. Wakefield said, coming into the kitchen with Mr. Wakefield behind her. The two of them joined the twins at the table. "You did an excellent job, Jessica. You, too, Elizabeth. I know that minding Chrissy was never easy, and it was often boring. I'm proud of you for sticking with it all week long."

Mr. Wakefield nodded. "Both of you girls did a wonderful job."

The Wakefields heard the front door slam, and a moment later Steven joined them in the kitchen.

"Hi, everybody," he said. "Hey, hot chocolate!"

Steven joined his family at the table. Mrs.

Wakefield sat back with a thoughtful look on her face. "You know, I've been thinking, Ned," she said. "Now that we've seen how well the twins can manage young children, maybe it's time to consider having another child."

Mr. Wakefield nodded. "You might be right, Alice," he replied. "The girls could be a lot of help—changing diapers, doing the laundry, baby-sitting. And from the way Steven pitched in with the kitchen chores, I'm sure he wouldn't mind running a few errands, helping to clean the house—"

"Oh, no!" Jessica and Elizabeth shouted at the same time.

"Another little kid around?" Steven asked. "No way!"

Mrs. Wakefield looked surprised. "But you were so eager to have Chrissy stay with us, Jessica. And Elizabeth, you mentioned how nice it would be to have a little brother or sister."

"One brother is enough," Jessica said, with a grin at Steven. "Another would definitely be *too* many."

Mr. Wakefield leaned over and tousled Jessica's hair. "We were just teasing," he said. "Your mother and I have enough to handle with *three* children, never mind four!"

Laughing, Elizabeth and Jessica hugged their parents.

"Now, confess," Mrs. Wakefield said. "Can I say 'I told you so'? Won't you be glad to see your 'little sister' go home again?"

Both twins nodded. Then Elizabeth smiled. "But you know," she said thoughtfully, "I *was* kind of sorry tonight when we sang 'Puff the Magic Dragon' to Chrissy for the last time."

At that moment, a sleepy voice came through the kitchen door. "I want a drink of water, 'Lizabeth," Chrissy announced.

Jessica laughed. "Well, Elizabeth, it looks like you'll get to sing it one more time!"

The twins met Amy and Mandy on the way to school Monday morning.

"How did your parents like the soccer game, Amy?" Elizabeth asked.

"They loved it!" Amy answered. "My dad is nuts about soccer, and my mom gave me a complete play-by-play when she got home." She grinned. "But if I ever think of doing something like that again, will one of you guys remind me of last week's disasters?"

"Speaking of disasters," Mandy said, "was Chrissy glad to see her parents on Saturday?"

Jessica laughed. "She was almost as glad as we were."

"Hey," Amy said as they turned the corner

toward school, "remember that girl who came to visit our school with her mother? Mr. Bowman told me her parents decided to enroll her."

"Really? That's great," Elizabeth said.

Jessica frowned. "What girl? I didn't see anyone."

"That's right. You came to class late the day she was visiting. Her name is Maria," Amy said, "and she'll be in the sixth grade."

"I saw her, too," Mandy said, "and I thought her clothes were really funky."

"Me, too. And she's pretty," Elizabeth added.

"You know, I remember thinking I'd seen her someplace before. I know I never met her, but still, she looked familiar," Amy said.

Jessica stopped in her tracks and put her hands on her hips. "Why do you guys know so much about her? Why didn't *I* see her?"

Elizabeth shrugged. "I don't know, Jess. I guess you just weren't in the right place at the right time. And," she added with a smile, "if you'd come to class on time . . ."

"It's not fair," Jessica insisted. "*I'm* the most popular girl in Sweet Valley Middle School and *I* should know about any new kid, particularly one who wears funky clothes."

"Take it easy, Jess," Amy said. "You sound like Chrissy!"

"Yeah, Jess. You'll get to meet her soon enough. And then you can give her an official Unicorn welcome!" Mandy grabbed Jessica's hand and pulled her along the sidewalk. "Come on. Let's not be late for school. Who knows what other fascinating people you might miss!"

***Will Jessica become friends with the new girl in town? Find out in Sweet Valley Twins #50,* JESSICA AND THE SECRET STAR.**